The SILENT Author

Russell F. Moran

The Silent Author

Coddington Press

Copyright © 2020 by Russell F. Moran

www.morancom.com

Printed in the United States of America

ISBN-978-1-7338872-4-3

Covers and text design by LuAnn T. Palazzo
www.PalazzoDM.com

DEDICATION
This book is dedicated to the novelists of the world.

ACKNOWLEDGEMENTS

As always, I thank my wife, Lynda, for her attentive reading, rereading, and editing of my many drafts, and for laughing at my jokes. Lynda is to me as Melanie is to Max. I also thank my friend and editor, John White, for his keen editorial eye. I thank LuAnn T. Palazzo for her expert interior and cover designs. And I especially thank my readers, many of whom are a constant source of inspiration and encouragement for me.

AUTHOR'S NOTE

The Silent Author is the story of writer Melanie Pierce and her husband FBI Agent, Max Wakefield. Melanie and Max are two of my favorite characters, and I think of them as old friends. As I wrote this book, we took a lot of adventures together. I hope you will see them that way too.

You will find a **Cast of Characters** after the last chapter of the book. It can be frustrating to come across a character on page 150, that you first met on page 20, especially if you've put the book down for a few days. I've seen this done in Russian literature, and I happily add a cast of characters to *The Silent Author* as well as my other novels.

Chapter 1

I feel terrible for my girls. They depend on my fees, but now I'm broke. Yesterday I was quite wealthy, if you consider $20 million wealthy. I think that's a nice amount of money—but it isn't so nice when it goes missing.

Today, all my investment and bank accounts are gone. My 15 girls, average age 82, are my good friends and beta readers. That's right, beta readers, meaning that they review all of my books before my final draft, sort of like informal editors. They all have the same thing in common. They are widowed with no children to help them and very little income or savings, just like my late aunt Jessie, a sweetheart if there ever was one. A typical beta reader doesn't get paid but works voluntarily. Not my girls. I love what they do for me and I put my money where my mouth is. Something deep in my gut tells me to take care of them, and I do, or at least I did. None of them are professional editors, but that's fine. They are extremely diligent and focused, and pick up small mistakes that I miss on rereads. They give me feedback from an average reader's point of view, which I think is the most important point of view. They are all good at spotting homonyms, words that sound alike but have different meanings and spelling, like "their, they're, and there." Writers, even experienced ones like me, often miss those simple things. Some of them even question substantive issues, such as pointing out when my plot goes awry, and that's a gift. Old Maggie Braxton, age 91, has severe dementia and can't read a word, but that's okay. She was one of my original girls and she needs the income to afford the excellent nursing home I got her into. For the modest amount of work they do, I pay them a crazy amount of money, which I'm happy to do. It makes their lives easier and it makes my books better. They each earn $10,000 for every manuscript, which works out well for them because I'm kind of prolific as an author, cranking out a book every two months. So, each of my girls earns about $60,000 a year for reviewing a manuscript every two months. Meg Trumbell, age 86, absolutely loves to beta read my books. She insists that she wants to do it for nothing because she enjoys it so much. I wouldn't hear of it, of course, and she gets her ten grand per manuscript just like all the others. My fees come with no strings so she can give it away if she likes. Knowing Meg, she probably does give it away to someone less fortunate. The editor at my publishing company loves that I submit a manuscript that's almost free of errors. I'm also a pretty good writer, I must admit. Each of the 25 books I've written has made *The New York Times* best seller list. An op-ed page article in the *Times*, written by the editor in chief, was titled, "Melanie Pierce, a Gifted Novelist for the Modern World." That was really sweet. It also made for a great blurb on the cover of my books. This week, two of my books are on the *Times* top 10 list. And I'm only 34 years old. Writing fiction is a shitty way to make a living, if you ever *do* make a living, but I'm one of the few who has discovered the key. Learn the basics, write good stuff, and keep your readers wanting for more. A little native talent helps, and I think I have it. I wrote my first novel in my senior year in college, and since then it's been my full-time occupation, a very remunerative one as long as nobody steals my money. I'm happy to say that my name rings bells in the publishing industry. If I can be pigeonholed into a genre, I guess my books could all be described as romantic thrillers. Jack Melton, my literary agent, couldn't be happier, and quite a bit richer. Surprisingly, 40 percent of my readers are men.

I love what I do, and I love my girls.

My favorite girl is my mom, Hedda Pierce. People tell me we're so much alike we could be twins. I love to hear that, because at the age of 58 she really is a doll. She's tall, at 5'11," slender, smart, and pretty. I also get my wiseass sense of humor from her. Whenever I need to come up with a funny crack, I channel Mom. Like me, Mom is into the arts and owns a successful gallery on Madison Avenue, which she and Dad started 30 years ago. Dad passed away eight years ago from cancer at the age of 50, and I still miss him. Mom is also one of my beta readers, although she isn't officially one of "my girls." I don't pay her, and she doesn't need it because her gallery rakes in tons of money. But she is probably my sharpest critic—and the funniest. Whenever she rips into one of my errors, she laces it with so much humor I don't know whether to laugh or cry. Just this morning I read one of her comments which said, "The lead character in this book isn't made of wood—he's made of stone, with all due apologies to rocks." I'm the only one who reads the comments, so they're never nasty, just private jokes between her and me. Mom is so insanely proud of my success that she showcases all my books in her gallery in a prominent display. Selling novels in an art gallery isn't common, but it gives Mom the opportunity to brag about me. She donates the income from the sale of my books to a scholarship fund for underprivileged writers. Like I said, she's a doll, in every sense of the word.

I walked over to my living room window, which has a commanding view of Central Park. Today is April 20, and springtime is starting to assert itself, adding to the pretty view with flowers starting to bloom. I love springtime, with its promise of renewal. But shit, I didn't feel renewed after having lost my money. I decided to stop looking at the view and get to work trying to get a handle on what happened to me.

I spent two hours on the phone with my bank and the managers of my investment accounts. I'm still trying to come to grips with the reality that I've been financially wiped out. And I've definitely been ripped off, big time. Fortunately, I still have a healthy current income from my royalties, but not enough to support my 15 girls and me. All of the withdrawals were over my signature, along with my usernames, account numbers, and passwords. That all pointed in one direction—Harry Paxton, my "boyfriend."

I call him my boyfriend, for lack of a better term. I'd been seeing Harry for two years after the sudden death of my husband, John, in a car accident. John and I had dated for 10 years, ever since we graduated from college together. We married four years ago and managed to put together a solid marriage, one full of closeness, love, and warmth. Mom loved him to pieces, and so did I. But then he was gone, just like that. I missed him so much I thought I'd lose my mind and almost did. When someone you love suddenly disappears, it turns your life upside down. At Mom's urging I began to see a psychotherapist. She worried that I'd commit suicide, and I must admit that I considered it. John's death hit me that hard. Marjorie Johnston, my therapist, was and is a terrific lady. She gently refused to put up with my bullshit, which takes some effort. I told her that I never wanted to be with another man, but she didn't buy it. I've never been much for the dating scene after John died, although I've been told that I'm not hard to look at. So, I didn't date, and I was lonely as hell. I missed John terribly.

Harry seemed to fill the bill for loneliness—sort of. We met in a bookstore of all places. He struck up a conversation about a book I was looking at, a book titled *Investing for Dummies*, a subject on which I needed some work. He invited me to have a cup of coffee at a luncheonette a couple of doors away from the bookstore. He told me that he was an "investment counselor," and blathered on and on about matters about which I knew little, but he seemed to know what he was talking about. We began to hang around, having lunch occasionally. He gradually became my "investment counselor," although he seemed to want a closer relationship. He suggested that we move in together, which didn't interest me at all. Although we dated, we never had sex. No way in hell could he replace John. Mom hated him, and that should have given me a hint that my companion-choosing skills needed some work. Although Harry and I weren't close, we talked often and that seemed to help with my loneliness. I noticed that I gave up on men since John died. After him, men just didn't interest me, especially Harry. My friends tell me that I'm quite good looking and they notice that men seem to fall all over themselves around me. I'm hit on so often I feel like a punching bag.

But their amorous advances did nothing for me. Harry, of course, was a man, and I honestly couldn't give a shit about him except for our occasional investment conversations. But where the hell is he? I called his landline phone for the umpteenth time. No answer. Then I called his cell phone again. The same. Next, I called Sheila Jackson, my best friend. I think of Sheila as my BFF (Best Friend Forever). She's right up there with Mom on my list of favorite people. Sheila is a freelance technical and scientific editor and works out of her apartment like I do. She's my age and we hit it off ever since we first met in college. Sheila's more like a sister than a friend. She and her husband, Chuck, would often double date with John and me. Sheila has an amazing way of sorting through complicated problems. I guess that has something to do with her scientific brain. I often bounce a scene off her from a book I'm working on. Even though she edits technical and scientific stuff, she has a great eye for fiction. Although she's not officially one of "my girls," I value her editorial comments.

After a few minutes on the phone with her, during which I explained my financial predicament, she said, "I'll call you back shortly." Sheila isn't one for wasting time. Pure energy, that one.

Forty-five minutes later she called me. "I drove by his house in Queens twice," Sheila said, "and neither of his cars were in the driveway. That's odd, I thought. He works out of his house as an 'investment counselor,' which I always thought was bullshit." Sheila liked Harry as much as Mom did. "The second time I drove by I stopped and rang the doorbell. No answer. I looked through a few windows and get this—the house is empty. You heard me, *empty*. Not a stick of furniture. Mel, honey, I'm afraid you've been fucked. I never did trust that bastard, and it looks like my suspicions were on target."

"Holy shit. Do you think that son of a bitch wiped me out?"

Rhetorical question. It was pretty obvious that Harry raided my assets.

I never felt close to Harry, just somewhat liked him. Somewhat. He had a pleasant personality, and his company made the time go by. Losing a wonderful husband like John at a young age can make you do stupid things. Looks like my trusting ways have gotten me into big-time trouble. Memo to file: *When your Mom and your BFF talk, you should fucking listen.*

"I'd better call the police," I said.

"Forget the cops," Sheila said. "this case involves theft from government accounts, not to mention funds crossing state lines, giving the federal government jurisdiction. Call my cousin, Max Wakefield, at the FBI. He'll know what to do about this crap."

"Isn't he that guy you've been trying to fix me up with?"

"The one and only. Hey, he's single, lonely, and incredibly handsome. He also has a heart of gold. There are few people in the world I trust more than Max. Too bad it takes a crime to get you two to meet, but he's definitely the guy to call. Max knows his shit. I'll call him on his cell to give him a heads up."

"God bless you, Sheila. I'll call him within the hour."

Yes, Sheila had been trying to fix me up with this guy for months, and even enlisted Mom in her matchmaking campaign. According to her, he's single, was engaged once but it broke off before marriage. I wondered what that was about. She also said that he was a veteran of the Marine Corps, a highly decorated captain no less. She also went on and on about his expertise as an FBI agent, mentioning a lot of newspaper articles about him. She also told me that he's a really nice guy, and good-looking to a fault. But I kept fending off Sheila's matchmaking efforts. I guess it was because of some kind of loyalty to "my boyfriend," that son of a bitch who wiped me out. Loyalty got me far—far into debt. I guess it's time to find out who this FBI guy is. Okay, he's a man, and I have absolutely no interest in men, especially after that bastard, Harry Paxton. Yes, I have no interest in men. None whatsoever. Been there, done that.

"Agent Max Wakefield, may I help you?"

"Agent Wakefield, my name is Melanie Pierce. Your cousin, Sheila, suggested I call you."

"Oh, hi. I just spoke to Sheila and she gave me a bit of the background on your case. Sounds like you're in serious trouble. May I come over to meet with you now? I'm about 20 minutes away from your apartment."

"That would be great. I'll be waiting for you."

He had a pleasant, friendly voice, which was a good thing because I had no patience for putting up with some tough cop bullshit.

A half hour later the doorbell rang, and I was shocked when I opened it. Holy shit, Sheila was right. This guy is incredibly handsome. He's about 6'3", broad shouldered with a slim waist. His ocean blue eyes can only be described as gorgeous. He had a smile that could melt ice. I took a deep breath and extended my hand, which he gently took in both of his. *Both hands!* I led him into the kitchen, my knees knocking. I had to remind myself that I have no interest in men. Absolutely. No. Interest. But it couldn't hurt to look.

"Coffee, Agent Wakefield?"

"I'd love some, and please call me Max."

We walked into the living room with our coffee and he sat on the couch, with me in the nearby chair facing him. Dear Lord, this guy's good looking. Okay, time to get down to business. But there's nothing wrong with looking at his heart-stopping face while we talk. I kept reminding myself, *I don't care about men. I don't care about men, I don't care about men.*

"Sheila told me that your investment and bank accounts have been raided and emptied. She said that you've lost over $20 million."

"Yes, I'm embarrassed to say that I'm quite loaded—or was."

"Don't be embarrassed. Melanie. You're a fabulous author, one of the best in the country, maybe *the* best, and you've earned every well-deserved penny of your money."

My God, what a pleasant guy. It's a good thing that men don't interest me.

"So, you're familiar with my work?"

"Yes, more than familiar. I've read every one of your 25 books—twice."

To say I was blown away would be a vast understatement.

"Oh my God, Agent Wakefield, so I'm sitting here with a fan?"

"Max."

"Oh right, Max."

"Yes, Melanie, I'm definitely a fan. You are one hell of a writer. I'm not exaggerating when I say that you're my favorite author. You have a way with words and thoughts that I find amazing and totally engrossing."

Could this be polite bullshit, or maybe an imaginative way of flirting? I figured I'd give him a quiz.

"How did you like *A Bullet Too Far*?" (a book I wrote a couple of years ago.)

"Oh, yeah, that great detective love story. Jack and Marjorie, if I recall their names, were partnered as detectives and hated each other. Then they started to like each other. Then, by the end of the book, they fell madly in love and got married. Great ending and one of your best books."

I have a hard time speaking with my mouth hanging open, so I just sat there silent for a few moments. Wow, this guy loves to read my books. He suddenly earned a spot on my favorite people list. I have no interest in men, but there's nothing wrong with a pleasant acquaintance. Is there?

He reached over to an end table, grabbed one of my books and turned it around.

"I've always thought that the photo of you on the back cover looked great, but now that I see you in person, the photo doesn't hold a candle. You're beautiful, Melanie, drop-dead beautiful."

My heart started pounding. I never expected a criminal investigation to be so friendly. Now, I don't know what to expect, but it's starting to look interesting. I've been with this guy, what, 20 minutes, and I'm getting to feel comfortable with him. Extremely comfortable. I mean, holy shit, he thinks I'm "drop-dead beautiful."

"Hey, Melanie, it's been my experience that talented people tend to be easily swayed by someone giving them praise. This could have something to do with your being defrauded. Somebody earned your trust and then wiped out your assets when you weren't looking. So, let me try some flattery on you as a mental game and see where it goes. Okay, here it is: 'You're a gifted writer, one of the best. Your words grab my heart and my brain.' So, give me your gut reaction to my flattery?"

"Let's run away and get married," my wiseass mouth said. Mom would have made a crack like that.

He let go of a booming laugh. "Sheila told me you've got a great sense of humor, and you just showed it. I'll leave your marriage proposal on hold for the time being." I enjoyed his laugh. It's loud, hearty, and lets you know that you've gotten to him.

He gave me a wink with one of his gorgeous blue eyes when he said that. I took yet another deep breath. I have no interest in men, but there's something about this guy, as my fluttering stomach noticed.

"So, getting back to your case, tell me about your suspicions."

"Only one person had my usernames, account numbers, and passwords, which I gave to him because he supposedly is an 'investment counselor.' But that's the only evidence I can give you, other than his name, Harry Paxton. From my research and writing, I know quite a bit about police procedure, and I have no direct evidence of any crime."

"From reading your books, I know that your knowledge of police procedure is stunning, Melanie. Besides being a fabulous writer, you're one hell of a researcher."

Shit, I'm starting to like this guy. He's a big fan of my books, he's sweet and polite, and he's killer gorgeous. What's not to like? Okay he's a man, a part of the species I've chosen to ignore. But he's a federal agent and he's working on my case, so I should pay attention. Right?

"But, even in the absence of actual fingerprints, Melanie, we have a huge set of facts staring us in the face. One day your accounts are wiped out and the next day your boyfriend goes missing, the only person who had access to all your login data. Oh, is it okay for me to refer to him as your boyfriend?"

"Lowlife scumbag would be more accurate, but why don't we just refer to him as Harry Paxton?" Lowlife scumbag was Mom's favorite name for him.

"Agreed. Hey, I must be going. We'll be talking a lot more in the near future."

Goddammit, no way in hell did I want our meeting to be over. I was having a really nice feeling talking to this guy, extremely nice, and something in the way he looked at me told me he felt the same. I'm starting to question my decision to swear off men. Maybe I can make an exception for *this* man. *Stay put, dammit, I enjoy talking to you.*

"How about another cup of coffee, Max?" I asked, trying to hit the brakes with both feet.

"I've already had two. One more and I'll get caffeine shakes."

"Then how about decaf?" I *really* didn't want him to leave.

"Yes, decaf would be nice." I don't think he was in a hurry to leave either.

"I can't believe I'm sitting here with my favorite author, and I'll be working your case."

I opened my desk drawer and took out a book. "Here's a copy of my latest novel. It will hit the stands tomorrow. Let me sign it for you."

"I can't accept a gift from a witness in a criminal case, but thanks anyway."

"Hey, snap out of it. This gift will be my little secret. The next time I see you there will be a quiz, so I suggest you get started on it." I felt like I was talking to an old friend, an intoxicatingly handsome old friend.

The sun was going down, bathing Central Park in a golden light. It gave me a feeling of warmth. But the setting sun wasn't the only warmth I was feeling. *Hold on, get a grip, slow down.*

"There's another thing I need to ask you about, Melanie. Sheila told me about a group of women you refer to as 'my girls.' Can you tell me about them?"

"Yes, they're 15 sweet old ladies who I've taken on as a sort of project. I've always been fond of elderly women, and these gals definitely need help. To make them feel like they're not receiving charity, I ask them to review each of my books as sort of beta readers, informal editors, and they do a damn good job. That's the major thing I hate about having my money stolen. My girls will be without my fees for a while."

"Wow, Melanie. Sheila told me that you're a good person. She says that you're the 'real deal,' as she put it. I gotta say, you impress me with your kindness. Very few people would do what you do for 'your girls.'"

He wrapped those beautiful eyes around me as he said that.

Oh, my God, I suddenly realized something. Max reminds me of John, my wonderful John. Just like John, he's Hollywood handsome and sweet as pie. Could that have something to do with my heart pounding like a jackhammer? My aversion to men is definitely on hold, at least it is with this guy.

Our meeting finally came to an end, not that I wanted it to, and I don't think he wanted it to end either. He reached over and handed me his card.

"Melanie, if you have any questions at all, or even if you just want to see me, just give me a call." He flashed his heart-stopping smile when he said that.

"I will, Max." My God, will I ever.

Chapter 2

The following evening my phone rang around seven. I had just spent the past four hours working on my latest book.

"Hi, Melanie, it's Max. I just wanted to ask you a few questions for my investigation. I hope I'm not interrupting dinner."

He *was* interrupting dinner, which I had just placed on the table. Suddenly I had no interest in food, even though I was hungry. Talking to Max seemed like a much better idea than eating. I noshed on a piece of celery, holding my hand over the mouthpiece so he couldn't hear my crunching.

He started with small talk, not investigator's questions but what could be best described as chit chat. Then the conversation continued with a lot of sharing of personal information. This wasn't an investigative interrogation, more like a couple of old friends shooting the shit. It seemed obvious to me that we both wanted to get to know each other better. I sure as hell was more than open to the idea.

I asked him how he got his start as an FBI agent. He told me he graduated from Georgetown University, and, after prompting from me, I learned that he was the star of the tennis team. He's my age, 34. He joined the FBI after serving as an officer in the Marine Corps.

"I've only played tennis a couple of times, and I'm really lousy at it. Maybe you can give me some lessons." I said that to be polite, but he took it seriously.

"I'd be happy to give you some tennis lessons, Melanie. It will be fun."

Yes, fun. Really nice fun running around a tennis court with this hunk of a man in shorts and a T-shirt. *Okay, stop.*

After college he entered the Marine Corps and served in Afghanistan, where he was awarded a bunch of decorations for valor, mustering out with the rank of captain. He didn't volunteer that information. I learned it when I Googled his name and did a couple of hours of research on him earlier. Hey, I know what I'm doing. He's one hell of a man, a God's honest war hero and an FBI super star, even though he has a sweet, polite sense of humility. I poured myself a glass of water, a tall glass. Why is my hand shaking?

Then he told me about his family. His folks live nearby in Connecticut and his two brothers and sister live in Manhattan. His older brothers run a successful insurance agency, and his younger sister is a detective with the NYPD, and they occasionally worked a case together. He mentioned that he'd like me to meet them. Oh, my God, he wants me to meet the family! Then he asked about my family. I talked about my Mom and my three sisters, two of whom are college teachers and the other a pediatrician. Mom will absolutely love this guy. *Stop, focus.*

The conversation got around to our hobbies. I told him that besides reading voraciously I love to run, clocking in at least five miles a day. I also work out regularly in the small exercise room in my apartment. He commented that my running and workouts are probably the reasons for my beautiful body. Yes, he thinks my body is beautiful. I took yet another deep breath as I looked in the mirror. Beautiful? If he thinks so, that's more than fine with me. As we spoke, I took my running shoes out of the closet and put them by the door as a reminder to run tomorrow morning.

His main hobby, besides tennis, is shooting pool. He also likes to read (especially my novels). When I told him I only played billiards once, he volunteered to give me lessons, on top of my tennis lessons. I pictured his muscular arms wrapped around me as he showed me how to strike a pool ball. Oh my God, where is my mind going?

I can't remember the last time I enjoyed a phone call so much. We continued to talk, discussing our favorite movies and plays. So much for a criminal investigation.

Something was gnawing at my brain, and when something gnaws at me, I simply have to feed it. How am I going to ask this question without appearing like a snoopy flirt? Screw it, I'll just ask and see where it goes.

"Max, Sheila once mentioned to me that you were engaged once. I don't mean to pry, but do you mind me asking you about that?" Bullshit, I had every intention of prying. I needed to find out about this part of his past or no way in hell was I going to get any sleep tonight.

"Yes, Melanie, I was engaged to be married. I had just finished my second tour in Afghanistan and returned home. My fiancé told me she had made other plans. I'll say she made other plans. She married another guy while I was deployed."

I was stunned.

"So, this unpatriotic bitch left you standing at the altar and ran off with another man while you risked your life to defend our country?"

Sometimes my filter-free mouth takes off on its own. This was one of those times.

"God's honest truth, Melanie, I was devastated. But then I realized that war can do strange things to people, no less to relationships. When you're in the field under fire, you sometimes lose your ability to communicate the way you should. So, I was in the field for a year, and sometimes in a combat zone for weeks on end, and I couldn't answer her emails. Well, I guess I could have, but it's hard to concentrate on correspondence when you're under fire. She was a lovely woman and deserved a man who not only cared but *showed* that he cared. I'm afraid that I fell down on that job. By sheer happenstance I bumped into her and her husband one day while I was shopping. It was an uncomfortable meeting to say the least. But she took the stress out of our encounter and immediately introduced me to her husband, all the time smiling. She was, and still is, a beautiful, charming woman with a lot of heart, and her husband seemed like a hell of a nice guy. I wished them all the best for their future and meant every word of it."

"Oh my God, Max, Sheila told me a lot about you. So, there you were, a war hero just returned after serving your country and faced a woman who jilted you and got married. And all you say about her and her husband is what nice people they are. You had every right to feel anger and think of revenge. But no, you confronted the situation with amazing care and forgiveness. Your cousin Sheila is really crazy about you, and I can see why."

I couldn't believe I just said that but screw it. Something inside me said it was no time to edit my thoughts and feelings about this guy. At that very moment I decided to abandon my idea to avoid men. No way in hell do I intend to avoid this guy, this kind, handsome, sweetheart of a man.

"Hey, Melanie, I really should hit the sack. I've had a long day and I'm beat."

I looked at the clock. Holy shit, we'd been on the phone for two and a half hours, like a couple of teenagers yacking on a Wednesday night. His questions about my case never did come up.

"I enjoyed talking to you, Melanie. It's been a nice chat. Remember, any time you want to see me about something, my door is always open."

Nice chat? How about a friggin wonderful chat? After I hung up, I stared out the window and reviewed our conversation in my racing brain. Something is going on. Something is definitely going on—between us.

I was suddenly gripped with a combination of sadness and happiness. John, my wonderful John, would have really liked this guy.

Chapter 3

A Ms. Melanie Pierce is here to see you, Max. I don't believe she has an appointment."

"That's okay, show her in."

"Melanie, so nice to see you again. Wow, it's been only a few hours since we last spoke."

He flashed a heart-stopping smile and winked when he said that. This guy's face should require a legal permit. I sat on a nearby chair so my buckling knees wouldn't dump me on the floor.

"So, what can I do for you, hon, I mean Melanie."

Hon? He called me hon. I liked that—a lot, even though he took it back.

"You said I could drop by if I wanted to see you."

"Sure, so what did you want to see me about?"

"About nothing. I just wanted to see you. So, here I am." Yes, Mom definitely raised a wiseass.

He looked at me, smiling his sinfully gorgeous smile, but he appeared a bit confused.

"So, how about...?" he began to say, then he sneezed. I wondered if that's a nervous habit. I sure as hell was nervous.

"An early lunch?" I said, completing his sentence, whether or not it's what he intended to say.

"Wonderful idea. The treat's on me."

"Let's split it."

"But I thought you were broke?"

"My assets have been swept away, but I still have a healthy income from my royalties. I can't think of a better way to spend money than lunch with you." Holy crap, where is my mouth going? It seems that when I'm with Max, it just goes where it wants to. After our phone conversation last night, I've simply given up trying to control my words around this guy. I think I'm in trouble. And I kind of like it.

"So, Max. is this a date?"

"Let's just call it a working lunch."

Bullshit. This is a date, or at least it is to me.

We walked into the Big Case, a lunch place two blocks from 26 Federal Plaza. We sat at a small table in the back.

"Mellie, I have some important stuff to tell you about your case, things I didn't get to in our chat last night, but I don't want to talk here. We'll go over it back in my office." He called me Mellie, not Melanie. I don't know why, but his calling me Mellie caused a flame to flicker in my stomach. It sounded friendly, close, affectionate. Holy shit, what's going on?

Cool. He wants to talk more in his office. Our time together will be extended.

"So, we won't talk business, here," I said. "That's fine with me. You're a real professional as Sheila told me. Hey, Max. I'm about to embarrass myself, but there's something I've been meaning to tell you, especially after our endless phone call last night. I find you to be a really nice guy, somebody who I enjoy spending time with." Was I being too forward? Fuck it, just follow what's happening as it happens. I wanted this guy to know how I was beginning to feel about him. And I was definitely starting to feel things about him. Nice things. Warm things.

He blushed, his face turning beet read. He looked so adorable I wanted to jump over the table wrap my arms around him. Later. Maybe.

After lunch we walked back to 26 Federal Plaza to meet in his office. As we walked, I turned to him and said, "Hey, Max, do you notice something?"

"Notice what?"

"We're holding hands."

He looked at me and flashed a dazzling smile. My heart melted, as usual.

"Yeah, I guess we are holding hands. It feels kind of nice."

Wow, does it ever feel nice. I think I'm toast. Fucking well-done toast.

We walked into Max's office. He took his jacket off and hung it on a hook. My God, does he have a fabulous build. Six foot-three, broad shoulders, slim hips, and a cute little ass. My girlie wiggle was doing flips in my stomach. This guy was doing things with my brain and my insides.

"Mellie (*Mellie!*), because of the amount of money involved, your case is big, but suddenly it's gotten bigger. You're not the only woman novelist whose assets have been raided. There are ten other women authors who have lost substantial amounts of money in the past two weeks."

"Who are they, Max?"

"I don't mean to be coy, but I cannot give you that information right now. That's standard procedure in a criminal investigation. This case has suddenly gotten huge, and I'm the agent in charge of the entire investigation."

"So, I guess we'll be seeing each other quite often," I said softly, ignoring the irrelevance of my statement. I hoped he didn't hear it for what it was, an obvious flirtation.

"Yes, we will, Mellie. When can we get together again?"

"Tonight, my apartment, 6 p.m. I'll prepare dinner."

"I'll check my calendar."

"Screw the calendar. My place at six."

"Are you always this shy, Mellie?" he said, laughing.

"Yes, I am. See you later, handsome, I mean Max."

Chapter 4

So, I'm meeting tonight with my new FBI agent. This will be our third "meeting" in four days, counting our endless phone chat, and my stomach was doing triple flips. I felt like I was a 16-year-old girl. Nothing wrong with that. It was kind of fun being 16. What is it about this guy? I really don't know, but I'm willing to find out.

I prepared a light vegetable pasta with a side of salmon and shrimp. I added no garlic. I didn't want bad breath to interfere with something that may happen later. Please God, make something happen. Where the hell is my mind going? Nasty little secret places I realized. *Okay, stop this shit.* He's going to be here for the continuation of a criminal investigation. But the important thing is that he's going to be here. I'm a pretty good cook, and I think I did a great job with this dinner. I wanted to make him feel comfortable and welcome, but most importantly, I needed him to *know* that I want him to feel comfortable and welcome. *Oh, boy.*

At exactly six p.m. the doorbell rang. I guess FBI agents are used to being punctual.

He stood there wearing a sinfully smashing smile, holding a

bottle of wine and a bouquet of daisies.

How does he know I like daisies?

"How do you know I like daisies?"

"I noticed four daisy bouquets in your apartment when I was first here."

Wow, powerful talent for observation. I wonder if he observed that I was grinning like an idiot and perspiring.

He handed me the daisies and wine. I wish I had a video of the scene. He was tilting forward slightly and so was I. It was clear to me that we both wanted a kiss. Later. Yes, definitely later. Max took off his jacket and rolled up his sleeves to uncork the wine. My God, what muscular forearms. He noticed my noticing and smiled. I found myself making a mental list of things that make him smile. I can't get enough of that intoxicating smile. I think I'm done for.

As we ate, we chatted about everything. I find it easy to talk to this man, no forced speaking, just open talk like we've been pals forever, just like our marathon phone conversation the other night. As we ate, he constantly complimented me on my cooking. I don't know if he was just being polite, but I didn't care. Kind words from him were starting to mean a lot to me. A lot.

He helped me clean the table, putting the dinnerware into the dishwasher. As he reached around me with a plate, he rested his left hand on my shoulder. I looked up at him, our faces less than an inch apart. We stared into each other's eyes. He didn't remove his hand. I sensed that something was about to happen.

It happened.

He kissed me, a gentle soft kiss on my lips. I returned the serve, with embarrassing enthusiasm. We hugged each other and kissed a deep wonderful kiss that I never wanted to end. It was a friendly kiss, but a deep one, a kiss that conveyed a sweet message. Something told me that the kiss was the beginning of something, something wonderful. Oh, my goodness, I'm cooked. Totally fucking cooked.

"Hey, I'm really being too forward. After all, this is only our first date." Wow, he called it a date!

"No, Max, this is our fifth date. I'm counting your first interview with me as date number one, our long phone conversation as number two, our lunch as date number three, and the follow-up meeting in your office as date number four. So, this is date number five."

"I like your bookkeeping, Mellie. So, I guess I wasn't being too forward by kissing you."

He had his arms wrapped around me, and I noticed his hands making their way down my hips, and then gently caressing my ass. I thought my knees would collapse. He kissed me softly and rubbed his nose against mine.

I suddenly realized that I hadn't had sex in two years, the night before John died. A thought came crashing through my brain. *It's been too long—and now is the time, right now.*

"Is there anything else I can help you with, Mellie?" He was referring to the remaining dishes, I think. I didn't care what he was referring to. I needed to tell him something, something important.

"Yes, you can help me, Max. Make love to me. Take me to bed right now and let me show you how I feel about you."

So much for my shy novelist persona. I cannot friggin believe I invited him to bed. I can't believe it but I'm happy I did. This man was making me crazy. Nice crazy.

His beautiful arm muscles are backed with serious strength. He reached down and put his left arm around my legs and lifted me, carrying me to the bedroom as if I was light as a feather. He gently set me down on my feet at the edge of the bed and began to undress me. *Undress me*! I kicked off my shoes, wrapped my arms around his broad shoulders and let him continue. Then I began to undo his shirt, then loosen his belt buckle, then drop his pants. He gently undid my bra and tossed it on an end table. Then he bent over and pulled down my panties. We stood there, naked, our bodies so close to each other you couldn't tell where he stopped and I began.

He stepped back and looked at my body. "Mellie, you're irresistible, impossibly beautiful." Another kiss, another heavenly kiss. He gently picked me up and rested me on my back onto the bed. Then he climbed in next to me, kissing my neck and stroking my breasts. Then he reached down and his long fingers toyed with my happy trigger, driving me totally insane. His muscular body wrapped around me. I felt myself getting close as my hips surged to his. Oh my goodness was I ever getting close, and I sensed that he was too. Then it happened, a mind shattering, earth moving, mutual orgasm. We said each other's name as if we wanted to communicate that what just happened was all about each other. Yes, it was about each other.

Max Wakefield is it. He's the one.

We lay there with our arms around each other, happy and spent. Or at least I thought we were spent. Max rolled his beautiful muscular body on top of me and I felt him enter me again, hard as a rock. He slowly entered me back and forth and I matched his thrusts. Then he picked up speed, long wonderful bursts of speed. It seemed as if we were communicating—with our bodies. Again, we came to a jarring mutual climax. I can get used to this.

No, that's not so. I can *never* get used to this. As if to confirm my thinking, we made love yet again. All of a sudden, I didn't care that my money was stolen. That theft brought me together with this wonderful man. Worth every bit of $20 million.

At 5 a.m. we reluctantly got out of bed.

Still naked, I walked to the shower. I could feel his eyes on my body.

"Want company?" Max said.

"Yes."

We made love—again—under the warm shower. I told Max that his middle name should be stamina. He was insatiable, and so was I.

When we walked out of the shower, we grabbed a couple of towels and dried each other off. What is so sensual about drying off another person's body? I don't know, but I felt like I was about to explode with pleasure. I will never to forget our first night together—our first of many, please God. My memories will show up in future novels, but for now I want to keep writing this one.

Max said that he didn't bring a set of clothes and needed to go back to his place to change for work. I reminded him to bring an overnight bag for the next time.

"The next time?" Max said. "When will that be?"

"Tonight?"

"I'll be here."

We kissed at the door. I sensed that we both wanted to say something, but I held back. I wanted to say the three magic words to tell Max how I felt about him, but I didn't want the words to be confused with post-coital enthusiasm. I am totally nuts about this man, and I think that Max feels the same way about me. My God, after five dates I felt like I knew him forever. And I never want to let him go. I've never been one to rush into things, but with Max, I can't go fast enough. Yes, put the stove on simmer. I am totally well-done.

Soon, I'll tell him exactly what I feel for him. Soon.

Chapter 5

I went back to bed for some much-needed sleep after Max left. It sounds like a cliché, but I'd just spent a night in heaven, a night with Max. I'm 34 years old, old enough to know what life is about, and young enough to know what I want. Him, I want. I want Max Wakefield in my life.

I walked the four blocks to the Federal Plaza. I walked, but it wasn't easy walking after last night. My girly parts reminded me of our amazing night together. As usual, I didn't have an appointment, but too bad, I needed to complete something. A good novelist knows when a story has reached a turning point. It makes a reader want to continue flipping pages. And did I ever want to keep the pages flipping.

His assistant escorted me into his office. Max was seated at his desk, looking like he needed some sleep.

"Hey, Mellie. You look beautiful as usual, but you're not smiling. What's that about?"

"I'm not smiling because I have an important message for you. A serious message." He looked concerned.

"So, what is it, hon?" (I get goosebumps when he calls me *hon*.)

The turning point of the story had arrived.

"I love you, Max. That's my message. I'm drop dead crazy in love with you. After all the hours we've spent together, I feel like I've known you all my life. And I can't get enough of you." Then I smiled.

"Please stand up, Mellie."

"Sure, why?"

"Because I want to hug you."

He wrapped his muscular arms around me and gave me a warm, tight hug, accompanied by a brain twisting kiss. You could have dropped a bomb on me, but being hugged by Max made me feel safe.

"I love you too, Mellie. I'm insanely in love with you." Another kiss.

I felt like I just entered a new world, a wonderful new world. He just now said he loves me!

"So, I guess this makes us *an item*," I said, stroking his handsome face. I can't friggin believe it but I was crying.

"Oh my God, yes. Are we ever an item," he said as he gently wiped my tears away.

We kissed again, a seemingly nonstop kiss, not that I wanted it to stop. Federal Plaza may not be a romantic setting, but at that moment I felt like I was in heaven.

Max and Mellie are in love. We're *an item*.

Chapter 6

After our wonderful meeting, the meeting where we said we loved each other, Max had to run to a crime scene. I called Sheila to have lunch. We hadn't spoken in a few days and I had my normal need to bring her up to date on what's happening with me. We met at a place around the corner from her apartment. We sat in the back, the usual spot for our get-togethers. It was crowded, but the hum of voices made it easier for us to talk in private.

"So, I haven't spoken to you in a few days, Mel. I talked briefly to my cousin Max as we do once a week. My God, Max is one of the most articulate, well-spoken people I've ever met, but his tongue was wrapped around his ears every time your name came up, which it did often. Mel, that man is in love."

"Yes, I know. And so am I."

"Holy shit," Sheila yelled, causing a few heads to turn.

"And if it wasn't for my best buddy, Sheila, it never would have happened. You are officially my favorite matchmaker. I think I'll change your name to Yenta."

"So, tell me about it. I guess your meeting went well." Sheila always wants the full story.

"Our one meeting turned into five in six days. I think it's a thing called chemistry. I felt it percolating when I first laid eyes on him, and I know that he felt it too. Now I can't get enough of him. We told each other exactly how we feel, that we love each other. Sheila, he's the one."

"That story is so sweet I'll think of you two as my favorite candy. You're the M&Ms."

"M&Ms! I love it Sheila."

"He sure beats the hell out of the son of a bitch thief you were seeing. Is Max still on the criminal case?"

"Yes. Besides being a sweetheart, he's a hell of a diligent FBI agent. It seems that my case isn't the only one about an author being ripped off. I can't go into more detail than that, other than to say that Max is heading up the entire investigation."

"With Max on your side I wouldn't worry about a thing, Mel. Knowing my cousin, he'll make all that bad shit go away. Especially now because he loves you."

Chapter 7

That evening, after my lunch with Sheila, I called Mom. I was dying to tell her everything about Max, *my* Max, the man I love, the man who loves me. I was glad she was at home and not at the gallery because she screamed so loud, I thought the phone would crack. I can't wait for her to meet him.

"As you're aware, honey, Sheila had enlisted me in her matchmaking campaign, and I think I provided you a lot of encouragement. She sent me a photo of the man. My God, is he handsome. From what Sheila tells me he's a good guy as well. I think you'll find it easy to get over that lowlife scumbag who 'managed' your money."

"There's nothing for me to get over with Harry, Mom. The only thing between us was my money, which is now gone. God bless Sheila—and you, for getting me together with Max. Too bad I waited so long. Mom, I am totally in love with this guy. As I told Sheila, he actually reminds me of John, my wonderful John. I feel like I've gotten my life back together."

Mom cried. She's such a sweetheart and I know she's happy for me.

"Mel, honey, you should write a novel about this experience. I can almost feel a best seller on the way."

The next day Mom and I planned to have lunch at the Brooklyn Diner on 57th Street, one of my favorite eateries. Their corned beef is to die for. Typical of me, I love to weave a plot, so I asked Max to join me. I didn't tell him that Mom would be there, and I didn't tell Mom that Max would be there either. Nothing wrong with a little intrigue. As I do with my novels, I love to keep the pages turning.

Max walked in a few minutes after we got there, looking like a movie star in a starched Oxford blue shirt and trim khaki pants. He has such casual elegance on a manly body that he begs to be hugged.

"Mom, I'd like to introduce Max, the guy I can't seem to shut up about. Max, meet my mother, Hedda Pierce."

They both seemed shocked and happy to meet each other. Typical of Max, he totally charmed Mom, not with some put-on "charm the lady" routine, just Max, authentic, friendly Max, the real deal. The man I love.

They're both great conversationalists and seemed to really like each other, which made my heart flutter. We had a wonderful lunch. I couldn't help but imagine both our entire families getting together, maybe when we get engaged. Max hasn't popped the big question yet, but, knowing him, he's waiting for just the right romantic moment. If he doesn't I will. It will be the next chapter of our lives and we're writing it together.

What can possibly go wrong?

Chapter 8

Good morning, Ali. We have some wonderful matters to discuss." Mustaffa Creezin said to his friend, Ali Chudori. They met at Creezin's apartment in San'a, Yemen.

"Mustaffa, you should call me by my Gentile name, Harry Paxton. It's important to keep my cover on tight."

"Harry, you have performed even better than The Committee expected of you. Because of people like you, the *Silent Author Project* is going well."

Please tell me more about the *Silent Author Project*, Mustaffa. I knew my role, and I'm pleased to say that I carried it out well, but I'd like to know more about the project as a whole.

"The *Silent Author Project* is The Committee's idea to silence the heathen bitches who criticize Islam. After we empty their bank accounts, we secretly administer a drug that robs them of their mental faculties. We call the drug the *Veritas*. The drug is very powerful. To date, two of the authors have been administered the drug. They now show symptoms of advanced Alzheimer's disease. We have assigned other brothers like you, who are also talented actors. Our goal, besides silencing the women, is to steal their considerable assets to fund our project. As you know, our funds are low because of the feverish efforts of the FBI and CIA to stop us. You and our brothers are filling up the accounts with new money. Praise be to Allah, but your action with that bitch Melanie Pierce has been our best move to date. Most of her 25 books include a few passages denouncing Islam. No less than $20 million of new funds is now in our accounts, thanks to you."

"I was able to convince her that I was not only her friend and confidant, but her investment counsellor. I managed to get all of her usernames, account numbers, and passwords as you know. As the Infidels would say, she never knew what hit her. Is Melanie Pierce scheduled to be administered the *Veritas*?"

"Yes, we plan to infiltrate her apartment next week. We're sure she's had the locks changed, especially since that FBI agent is involved. Once we're inside, we'll inject the drug into her drinking liquids. Yes, soon her writing talents will be reduced to nothing."

"Do you know the FBI agent who is involved in the investigation?"

"Yes, his name is Maxwell Wakefield, a very diligent agent, one who has given us a lot of trouble in the past. Our spies tell us that he and Ms. Pierce may be dating."

Paxton laughed. "It will be interesting to see how Agent Wakefield reacts to dating a zombie."

Chapter 9

Dolores Hartman sat with her senior editor, Bill Randolph, at Hachette Book Group, her publisher. They met at the company's headquarters on Sixth Avenue in Manhattan.

The purpose of their meeting was to discuss the latest manuscript she handed in the week before. Dolores, age 39, is a best-selling author of thriller novels. She was a half hour late for their meeting because, for some reason, she forgot how to get to the office, even though it was only five blocks from her apartment, and she had been there countless times before.

"You look tired, Dolores, how about a cup of coffee?"

"Coffee would be nice. Squeeze in some lemon and pineapple, please."

He raised a confused eyebrow at her strange request and carried the tray to the table. "Here, you can administer your own fixings, Dolores."

She poured a glass of orange juice into her coffee, spilling it all over the desk.

"So, let's talk about *The Coming Storm*," Bill Randolph said as he wiped up the spilled coffee and orange juice.

"The coming what?"

"*The Coming Storm*, your latest submission."

"Oh yes, *The Coming Storm*," she said, a look of confusion on her face.

"I have a few observations and comments, Dolores, and I hope I'm not being too blunt." He took a sip of coffee, set it down, and entwined his fingers, still wet from mopping up the spilled coffee and orange juice. "First, about your characters. I find them very confusing. Some of them have differently spelled names in different chapters, and you provide no background information on any of them. It's hard to get to know the characters, much less want to follow them. They seem to be wooden stick figures with no personalities. Nothing about them draws the reader in, and you know how important that is. And about your grammar and punctuation. Of course, we put every manuscript through a few rounds of line editing, but we've grown accustomed to receiving work from you that's already highly polished. That doesn't describe this book. There's nothing polished about it, and it looks like a first draft. Definitely not like you, Dolores. Then comes the plot. It seems to meander all over the place with no coherent story line. Nothing seems to lead to the next scene. Also, the title you've chosen doesn't have anything to do with the story. You never answer the question that the title poses—what *is* the coming storm? Bottom line—I have no idea what the book is even about. I've known you for a long time, Dolores, and you're one of our best writers, and I think of you as a friend, not just an author. To be blunt, this submission is far below our standards. Hell, it's far below *your* standards. Any comments, Dolores?"
"Yes, when is the deadline for my submission?"

"It was last week, and you hit the submission date. That's what we've been talking about for the past half hour, your latest submission."

"Oh right, of course."

"Dolores, you sit right here, hon. Have some more coffee. I'll be back in a few minutes."

He went to the company medical office and returned to Dolores 10 minutes later with a physician's assistant in tow.

That afternoon, Dolores was admitted to NYU Langone Medical Center with a diagnosis of early onset dementia. *The Coming Storm* would never see the light of day.

Chapter 10

Hi, Mellie."

"Max, honey, I miss you." God's honest truth. I missed him like crazy. This man has totally infiltrated my brain and my heart. I've tried to stop thinking about him so I can get some writing done, but it doesn't seem to be happening. His name and his amazing face are always in front of me. This gorgeous man is definitely a new chapter in my life, a wonderful new chapter. After he met Mom yesterday, I felt even closer to him.

"Hey, it's only been 24 hours."

"Entirely too long."

"So how about tonight? Get dressed up nice. I want to take you to a special place later."

"What's the occasion?"

"It's a secret. But who needs an occasion for two lovers to celebrate? I'll be by at six to pick you up."

A secret? Could it be what I've been expecting? Please be

calm, tummy, while I freak out. Max has a secret and he wants me to dress up nice. Oh my God, am I in love.

I don't own a lot of sexy clothes, but I wanted to show Max a hint of what may come later. I put on a black dress, a couple of inches above my knees. It had a neckline that couldn't be described as plunging, but it definitely showed a bit of cleavage. My breasts are quite ample, and I wanted to remind him of that. This is so unlike me, but since I met Max, everything about me is different. My life is different.

At exactly six o'clock Max rang my doorbell. We exchanged a brief kiss to avoid painting Max's stunning face with lipstick, although that's what I felt like doing. Max stepped back and looked at my dress. The look on his face told me that I'd made a smart move to wear the only sexy dress I own, one that I looked forward to his helping me out of later. When we walked out the front door a limousine awaited us. A friggin limo! Max loves surprises.

The car pulled up to the building that housed The Four Seasons. My heart was pounding as Max squeezed my hand. The elevator took us to the restaurant floor which had a spectacular view of the city. The sky was clear, and a full moon bathed the city in a pleasant light. We were shown to a table with the best view. Max doesn't miss a trick. "So what's the secret, honey?"

"When I watch your pretty fingers work their magic on the keyboard, I realize that something is missing?"

"Like what?"

He reached into his jacket pocket and pulled out a jewelry box.

"A diamond ring is missing," he said as he slipped the beautiful stone on my ring finger.

"Marry me, Mellie. I want to be with you forever. Please say yes."

I put "shy Mellie" on hold, walked around the table, sat on his lap, wrapped my arms around his neck, and kissed him. I couldn't care less about what our fellow diners thought. If they felt the way I did, they'd understand.

"Forever is a nice amount of time, Max. The answer is yes, baby. Oh my God is the answer yes."

I wondered how many criminal investigations wound up like this. "On top of the world" is a worn-out phrase but screw it, I was on top of the world. I closed my eyes and envisioned us a few decades from now, still together and still in love.

The M&Ms are getting married. We'll be together—forever.

Chapter 11

At 2:30 on a Friday afternoon, Mark Longtree walked into Columbia Presbyterian Hospital. Although he wasn't related to the patient he went to visit, a nurse friend of his had given him a heads-up call. He got off at the fifth floor and walked to room 504. Rachel Cummings lay there in bed, the room otherwise unoccupied. Mark was a literary agent and Rachel was his best client. Under the title of her books she may as well write "Best Seller," because so many of them turned out to be just that. There was more to their relationship than agent and client. For the past few months, he noticed a budding love affair brewing between him and Rachel, a love affair he more than encouraged.

Although she looked tired, she was still beautiful, her light brown hair nestled around her face. Her eyes were closed. He leaned over and kissed her, waking her up.

She stared at him and smiled, although her face looked confused.

"My goodness, you're a nice-looking man," she said. "Who are you?"

"I'm Mark," he said, a tear streaming down his face. His nurse friend had told him that Rachel had been acting strange, and her question just proved it.

He reached over, stroked her face and said, "I'll be right back, honey."

"Honey? Is that my name?"

He went to the nurse's station where, fortunately, Dr. John Peterson, Rachel's attending physician stood, filling out a chart.

He introduced himself. The doctor, who seemed like a friendly guy, asked, "Are you related to the patient?"

"No, I'm not, but I'm her good friend and literary agent."

"Well, I should tell you that I can't discuss a patient with someone who's not a blood relative, but from the look on your face I think I'll get my jaw broken if I say that. Come over here and sit down on the bench with me, Mr. Longtree."

"Please call me Mark."

"Sure, Mark. This is a tough one, I've got to tell you. Your friend is only 36 years old, according to her records, but she's showing classic symptoms of dementia. When she was brought to the hospital earlier, she was wearing only one shoe and her dress was half off. Did she recognize you?"

"No, she didn't."

"That doesn't surprise me. She doesn't even know her own name. I've admitted her with a working diagnosis of early-onset dementia. I wish I had better news for you, Mark, but those are the facts. I've seen this before, but never in a patient so young. I'm a big fan of her books. You're lucky to have her as a client. She has such a fertile mind, but now she's acting like an Alzheimer's victim. Here's my card, Mark. Call me if you have any questions and I'll keep you up to date. Nothing would make me happier than to see that brilliant young woman hitting the best seller list again."

Mark walked back to Rachel's room. She was awake.

"Hi, my name is Honey," she said. "Who are you?"

Chapter 12

I was dying for Max to come to my apartment because I had a big surprise for him. I cannot believe that I'd forgotten to tell him about my waterfront vacation home in Amagansett on eastern Long Island. I'd been so busy with my writing and the investigation, not to mention my growing love affair with Max, that it had actually skipped my mind. I bought the place only three months ago, one of the few assets that my son-of-a-bitch "boyfriend" didn't steal. I had only stayed there once with my parents and sisters—without Harry the creep, fortunately. At least my mom and sisters got to enjoy the place often.

With my writer's flair for the dramatic, I made a three by three-foot poster of a photo of my Amagansett house and put it on an easel at the end of the dining room table. It was a beautiful aerial photo from a sales brochure when the place was on the market. I put a cloth over it to prepare the surprise.

At 6:05, Max walked in and we engaged in our usual hug and kiss.

"I've got a surprise, baby." I walked over to the easel and pulled off the cloth. I looked at Max, who was wearing a big smile.

"Let me guess," he said, grabbing my hand, "You've rented it and we're going to spend a weekend there. God, I love you."

"Better than that, honey. I own the place. It's in Amagansett right on the ocean as you can see. With all the excitement of the past couple of weeks I totally forgot to tell you about it. It's one of the few assets that my scumbag boyfriend didn't steal."

He hugged me, our usual way of communicating.

"I seem to have a hidden talent for picking the right girlfriend, not to mention the right fiancé. When are you going to show me the place?"

"Today's Thursday. Why don't we head there tomorrow and spend a long weekend on the ocean?"

"You're on, baby. Have I mentioned how much I love you? Making love to you with a view of the ocean sounds like a wonderful idea."

Early Friday morning, Max and I went to a nearby Hertz rental place to hire a car for our trek to Amagansett, a 107-mile journey from Manhattan. Amagansett is close to the eastern end of Long Island, right next to Montauk. Like most Manhattanites, neither of us owns a car. Much easier and cheaper to rent one when you need it, without having to worry about insurance and parking garage fees. Max and I are skilled at handling city life.

At 10:30 a.m. we pulled into the long driveway leading to my (our) house. Wow, I had forgotten how beautiful it is. The place sits on an acre of oceanfront property. The house is big at 5,000 square feet. On the ocean side of the house is a 20 by 40-foot swimming pool with a hot tub next to it. The design of the house is classic New England/Hamptons, sided with wood shingles.

The kitchen was immense and was combined with a great room. Excellent place for entertaining. Maybe I'll invite my girls for a weekend.

It had every kind of appliance imaginable. I enjoy cooking and looked forward to making some great meals for my honey and both our families.

Max and I had a blast walking around the house, most of which I had forgotten because I had only been there once. A warm, welcoming living room/den overlooked the Atlantic. The place came fully furnished and I couldn't imagine anything else we'd need. There were four complete *en suite* bedrooms, each equipped with a bathroom. The master suite included two bathrooms and had a fabulous view of the ocean. One of the bathrooms included a hot tub. Max pinched my ass as he ran his hand along the top of the hot tub.

I eyeballed a great spot for my writing with a lovely view of the ocean to put my brain into creation mode. Yes, I made a great move when I bought this place. Fortunately, my "boyfriend" didn't steal it.

We decided to take a dip in the pool. I wore a tiny red bikini I had just bought the day before. I've never been much for skimpy bathing suits, but with Max, everything is different. Making Max horny has become one of my favorite new pastimes. Max complimented me on my bikini as he helped me out of it. We forgot about swimming, opting instead for a much more exciting form of exercise. Max, as usual, drove me and my girlie parts insane.

On Sunday, Max gave me my first tennis lesson as he had promised. After 30 minutes, he walked up to the net and waved me over.

"Mellie, I can't believe it. After a few minutes you hit the ball like you've been playing all your life. I can't believe it, but you have a killer serve."

I'm quite athletic, I must admit. My father always called me "a born jock." I was happy that I found something else to enjoy with Max. We can't make love all the time. Well, not *all* the time. Max won the game but only by five points. After we played tennis, Max suggested we go into the den which housed a pool table that came with the house. He gave me a few pointers, wrapping his long, muscular arms around me as he demonstrated how to hit the ball. I recalled fantasizing about just that moment when we had our endless phone conversation a few weeks ago. I must admit that after we first discussed it, I had taken a few private lessons at a pool hall in Manhattan. Typical of me, when I discover a new pastime, I tend to go all in. After a few lessons, I think I could qualify as a pool hustler. Max challenged me to a game, unaware of my new-found skills. We took turns shooting a ball to see who would go first. I went first and "cleaned the table," sinking every ball. Max laughed and shook his head. "You have a wonderful habit of amazing me," he said. I think I'll include scenes of my tennis and billiard lessons in my next novel.

We decided to have Chinese food tonight. Actually, we ordered Asian fusion. My real estate broker told me about a great takeout place right in the hamlet of Amagansett. Nothing like a few pieces of sushi to fill your stomach without becoming bloated. Max and I both love sushi. When it was delivered, we sat at the kitchen counter and ate as we took in the view of the ocean. Using our chopsticks, we fed each other. I don't know why but feeding Max made me feel horny. But everything about Max makes me horny. As always, we talked nonstop.

Max has been recently been taking a serious interest in my writing, which makes me crazy happy. He's smart as hell and has a hidden talent for editing that he never knew he had. It probably is a result of his diligent work on FBI files. He spots things that I missed even after a few rounds of rewriting. He also has great suggestions for adding scenes. It's like he's tapped into my writer's brain and formed a tight connection, as if things could get any tighter between me and Max. Most writers I know prefer to be on their own, at least for the first few drafts. But with Max, I feel like he's part of my head, part of my writing, part of my life. His interest in my writing makes me feel closer to him, if that's even possible. The latest book I'm writing is a thriller, of course, but it's mainly a romance, a real love story. The chapter I want Max to look at is a love scene. I'm usually a bit tame when writing love scenes because I don't want a reputation as a closet porn writer, even though all my books contain a love story. But this scene was so steamy my keyboard felt hot. The reason it was so sexy was because it was based on my actual experiences, making love with Max. Like most of my stories, my life experience flowed out of me onto the keyboard. I didn't leave anything out, and the scene almost wrote itself. I closed my eyes and the words appeared in front of me. Max sat next to me on the couch as he read it while we sipped martinis.

"Wow, Mellie, this chapter is hot. If I close my eyes, I'm back there in bed with you, wrapped around your gorgeous body. But one thing I've noticed in my years as an investigator, it's always a good idea to rework the evidence to make sure you got it right."

"So, you think we should rework the evidence?" I said as I stroked his thigh, breathing in his wonderful cologne, which combined the scent of salt air with his manliness.

"Yes, I do. We want to make sure you didn't leave anything out," he said as he began to unbutton my blouse. "Let's go to the evidence room and make sure you got it right." He grabbed my hand and led me to the bedroom.

I realized that I just found my new favorite editor.

———— ⬥ ————

After we rehearsed a few more "scenes," we lay in bed next to each other, naked. I rested my right hand on his beautiful muscular chest as he read through a few more pages of my manuscript.

"Mellie, I can't believe the beauty of what I just read. Let me read it aloud."

Before she met him, she thought she knew what love was. Until then, she thought love was a warm feeling, a physical attraction, and maybe a bit of lust. He taught her differently. Love, as he taught her, was an all-consuming reality, a body and soul togetherness, an all-powerful desire to be with the person you love, and to give him your everything, your heart and soul.

"Mellie, your heart wrote those words didn't it?"

"Yes, it did, baby. My heart wrote those words because of you. You've taught me what love is, and I get to share it with the world through my writing. You've introduced me to a new life, honey—a life with you."

He set the manuscript on the end table and wrapped his arms around me. At that moment he showed me that my writing was more than just prose—it was an expression of my love for him.

Definitely my favorite editor.

Chapter 13

We drove back to my apartment in Manhattan on Monday afternoon, having just spent an unforgettable weekend in Amagansett. I can't count how many times we had sex, but I realized it was more than sex, as exciting as it was. When we made love, it was just that, *love*. As I said in one of my books that Max had just read, a book that was inspired by Max, *Love is an all-powerful desire to be with the person you love, and to give him your everything, your heart and soul*. That describes the love between Max and me. The sex is wonderful and exciting, but the love is everything.

Max wanted to go over with me some new parts of his investigation at home. I call it "home," because that's what my apartment had become, my home and Max's. We like to meet at my apartment because it's large and luxurious, with a great view of the city. There are now two favorite parts of my day: welcoming him home and waking up next to him in bed. God bless my BFF Sheila for leading me to this man.

We talked about setting a wedding date and both realized that his sudden large case load precluded any big plans. That's okay, we're getting plenty of practice being married. Plenty.

"I've been assigned three newly-hired agents to help me with this case. They may be new, but they're smart as hell. I've given them a research assignment I dreamed up. Their task is to read all the books that you and your fellow embezzled authors have written. They started two days ago. The guy who's been reading your books told me he's going nuts about your writing. You've got a new fan, Mellie, and I'm sure the next guy to start on your books will be one too. You are such a fabulous writer."

"You have a nice way of saying the sweetest things, Max."

"I may say sweet things, but they're also the truth. I love you and I love your writing. I think it's about time for a hug."

"It's always time for a hug."

I don't know what I did to deserve this man, but I better keep doing it.

"Any other writers being looked at right now?"

"Jacqueline Thompson. I'm sure you're familiar with her."

"Yes, Jackie and I are good friends and see each other often."

"Do you ever collaborate on what you're writing?"

"Never. We consider each other competitors. Good friends, but friendly competitors. We get together and flatter each other once we've published a book."

"God, you writers love flattery, don't you?"

"Yes, we do. So why don't you say something flattering, honey."

"You have the sexiest body God ever created. How's that?"

"Your flattery makes it easy for me to get excited, and for me to get *you* excited. Just thinking about you having an erection gets me all tingly."

"Hey, don't get me started, we have work to do."

"Okay, so have your readers noticed any similarities so far?"

"Yes, although we're still early with the project. I figure it will take at least a month for these guys to finish the books. With an author like you it's easy to read because your work is so great."

"Hey, stop with the flattery or I'll drag you to bed."

"Let's finish our conversation so I can take you up on just that."

"So—similarities?"

"The ABCs are picking up a lot of scenes about radical Islam."

"ABCs?"

"Yes, Al, Bob, and Charlie, the ABCs, our FBI readers. You and the other authors so far seem to be quite critical of Islam, extremely critical. Any observations about that, hon?"

"Speaking for myself, of course, yes, the radical fringes of Islam work well into a thriller, especially a thriller involving terrorism. Radical Islam and terror seem to go together. I have no problem with the religion of Islam, but I have a big problem with its radical fringes. They're creepy scumbags, just like the slimeball who wiped out my bank accounts."

"I hope you don't use the words 'creepy scumbags' in your books."

"I can't guarantee that I never do. I like to write about what it is, not what it may be."

We finished our discussion of my writing. I grabbed Max by the hand and led him to the bedroom so I could show him how much I enjoy his flattery. I think we use his flattery as an excuse to have sex. So what, who needs an excuse?

My goodness am I in love.

Chapter 14

Mellie, stay put. I'm coming right over."

"Looking for a little mid-day excitement?"

"Not the kind of excitement we'd like. I'll have a couple of other agents with me."

Twenty minutes later Max showed up with two other agents I'd met before, Bob McGraw and Nancy Buchannan. All three wore disguises, consisting of wigs and weird-looking glasses. What the hell is going on?

"Pack some clothes, honey. Nancy will help you."

"Pack clothes? Where are you taking me?"

"To a lovely place, a large apartment in the WPP?" From my writing I knew that WPP means the Witness Protection Program.

"Max, please explain."

"As you know, we've been tracking other best-selling women authors. Two of them had all their assets embezzled, but the worst part is that they were administered some kind of mind-altering drug. They're hospitalized and act like a couple of zombies. Our spies think the jihadis call the substance the *Veritas*."

"Who are they?"

"I'm sure you know them. Rachel Cummings and Dolores Hartman."

"Holy shit. Yes, I know them well from the Romance Writers Association. They're both best-selling authors. You say they've been drugged?"

"Yes, they've been drugged, and they both show the symptoms of early-onset dementia. Sad as hell for two women so young. That's why we need to get you into the Witness Protection Program. A lot of critics think you're the best novelist in the country, and I totally agree with them. I'm sure you're on the list of women they want to hit next with that *Veritas* drug, whoever the hell *they* are. Don't worry about the apartment. I've assigned two agents who will regularly check the place. The Federal Marshalls Service and the FBI are good at this WPP stuff. A personal shopper has been assigned to you, so don't worry about clothing and personal effects. Just pack what you need for the next day or two. A car awaits us. I'll go first, followed by you a few feet behind me. Bob and Nancy will follow you."

Then Max hugged me. I wasn't concerned about Bob and Nancy seeing this. Everybody at the Bureau knows that Max and I are "an item." I couldn't believe what's happening to me, but with Max by my side, I wasn't worried, just confused.

Max personally visited Mom to tell her about my new status as a guest of the Witness Protection Program. Mom loves Max and freaked out when we became engaged. Max loves her too. Only a sweetheart like him would make a personal visit to my mom to let her know what's going on. Mom wasn't too pleased that she couldn't visit me at my WPP apartment, but after Max explained everything to her, she gets it.

The car drove us a few blocks to a beautiful brownstone on Fifth Avenue and 68th Street a couple of blocks from the Central Park Zoo, a place I would often stroll around for inspiration. I also wore a disguise. My blond hair is now covered by a frizzy black wig and my fit body now looks like an overweight woman with all the padding under my clothing. I think I wrote about this in a novel I did a couple of years ago. Max whispered in my ear, "I can't wait to help you out of those clothes."

"How about right now?" I said.

"Hey, frisky lady, we have colleagues with us."

"You're the boss. Tell them to look the other way."

Max pinched my butt. He's gotten used to my wiseass comments.

The elevator took us to the fifth floor and Max led us to an apartment. Wow, I thought my place was nice, but this apartment was stunning. All the walls were done in light walnut paneling. The floors were all hardwood, a few of which were covered by oriental rugs. It had three bedrooms, one of which was a large master room with a king-sized bed and an attached large bathroom with a huge shower stall and a hot tub. We *love* hot tubs. Actually, we love anything that requires us to get naked. Max stroked my ass as I ran my hand over the bed. "You'll be entertaining a special guest quite often," he said. "Don't worry about the other agents. They get it. When I'm here, your bodyguard will be stationed in that seating area in the hallway, so we'll have the whole place to ourselves."

Bodyguard? Did he really say that? It gave me a creepy feeling to know that I've been assigned a bodyguard. We toured the entire apartment, which was large at 2,100 square feet. It also included a sizeable exercise room, even larger than the one in my apartment.

He then led me up a short stairway to the roof, which was a breathtaking place. It came equipped with a with a wrap-around running track, a well-tended garden, an outdoor eating area, and a hot tub. The track was perfect for my morning run. Every time Max compliments me on my "beautiful body," I resolve to keep it that way.

The entire roof was surrounded by large plexiglass windows. If the weather cooperated, I could live in the outdoor area.

"Don't worry, honey, all the windows. including the ones on the floor below, are bulletproof."

Bulletproof? Hearing that word made my stomach wince, almost as much as when he said the word bodyguard.

A month ago, I was a busy, wealthy author, happily working on my latest book. Now I'm living in the Witness Protection Program, my life in danger. I'm surrounded by bulletproof windows and bodyguards. The only thing that made it palatable was that I'd regularly see the best part of my life—Max.

Holding my hand, Max led me over to a large desk which faced the master window with a fabulous view of Central Park. The view faced east, making for afternoons of non-glaring sunshine, which is good because I do most of my writing in the afternoon, and sun glare just doesn't cut it. A lot of writers I know prefer to work without a view, finding it better not to be distracted. One of my writer friends actually works in a walk-in closet. I'm different. A beautiful view gives me ideas, feeds my imagination, creates scenes where my characters guide me through the story. My old apartment had a great view of a cityscape, but nothing like this. My "old" apartment? I wonder if I'll ever return there. One glance out the window of this place resulted in a new scene for a book I'm working on, a couple walking along a path through Central Park. The imaginary couple reminded me of me and Max, the M&Ms. I've noticed that characters inspired by Max are showing up more and more in my writing. Hell, he's in my life, the best part of my life. Why shouldn't he be in my books?

"Hey, Mellie, didn't you once tell me that you've thought about writing under a pseudonym, a pen name so to speak."

"Yes, my agent and I have kicked the idea around a lot. It opens doorways to experiment with different genres. Even a big-time author like J.K. Rowling writes under the pen name Robert Galbraith when she's not writing a *Harry Potter* book. We've been toying with the name Michael Hawkins. I've been thinking of writing a historical novel based in New York City, which will be a departure from my usual romantic crime thrillers. Yes, pen names can be useful. Why do you bring up the subject, honey?"

He handed me a small package which I opened. It was a brand-new iPhone.

"This will take some getting used to, Mellie, but Melanie Pierce no longer exists while you're in the WPP, except in her writing. Here's your new phone number, Mr. Hawkins."

The only people who still knew of my existence are my Mom, my good buddy, Sheila Jackson, my bodyguards, and Max.

Can my life get any weirder?

One thing really bothered me. Max and I are officially engaged, but now that I'm in the Witness Protection Program, when the hell would we become man and wife? Our lives together, certainly our sex lives, are as close as can be. But I want it to be official. I want Max to be my husband. I want the M&Ms to be one entity.

At 6:30 Max walked in, looking his sexy self. We greeted each other in our usual way. We kissed and hugged. We planned to have pizza tonight, and I was dying to share my thoughts with Max.

I waved my left hand in front of him, with the ring facing outward. "Pretty, no?"

"Pretty, yes," he said. "I must admit I have excellent taste in rings."

"Yes, you do, but something is missing."

"Like what?"

"Another ring next to it."

"Your mean a wedding ring?"

"That's exactly what I mean."

"Let's fix that right now," Max said. "God knows when you'll be out of this Witness Protection Program, Mellie. It's time to stop waiting. It will be a small wedding, but let's get married right here. How about this coming Saturday, two days from now? I'll call Father Rick Sampson. He's the pastor of St. Mark's Episcopal Church, the one we attend right here in Manhattan. I introduced you to him once if you recall. He's also an FBI chaplain, not to mention a great guy and a good friend of mine. I'm sure he'll jump at the chance."

This Saturday!? Max, God bless him, just like me he didn't want to slow things down. I thought my heart would jump out of my chest.

Max took out his phone and dialed Father Rick. He seemed to know the number by heart, telling me that Max isn't a stranger to religion, a believer like me. I cannot possibly live my life without this man. He and Father Rick chatted for a couple of minutes.

"Saturday at 11 it is, honey. I can't wait to call you my wife."

"In two days, you'll be my husband. We'll be joined in marriage. We'll be one entity. Oh, my God, I love you." We kissed, as usual, hugging each other as if we were afraid we'd float away.

"Hey, we've got planning to do," I said, then laughed. Actually, we have very little planning to do because the Witness Protection Program does not allow for large events. Max's friend and colleague from the FBI, Frank Bellone, agreed to be best man, and my BFF Sheila will be my maid of honor. Although she's not FBI, Max is totally okay with his cousin Sheila being in the wedding party. The guests will include four agents from Max's office and my two bodyguards from the Federal Marshalls Service. I asked Max to exercise whatever clout he had to get my mom invited to our wedding in the WPP. No way would I get married without my good pal, Mom. Max, of course, made it happen. The apartment came equipped with a grand piano, and Max says that Father Rick is a talented pianist, so we'll even have music. The FBI thinks of everything, so Max arranged for our personal shopper to get us wedding rings that we picked out of a catalog.

We discussed having a big formal wedding, including relatives and friends, when I get out of the Witness Protection Program, but for now it will be small, very small.

Saturday, the day of our wedding, arrived. I was so happy I thought I'd pee my pants. My fiancé is about to become my husband.

The wedding ceremony took place in the rooftop garden on

a beautiful day in May. When Father Rick said, "You may kiss the bride," I thought my heart would burst with love. It's not like we aren't used to kissing, but now I kissed my husband, my other half, my better half, the man of my life.

After the ceremony, we walked down to the huge den, where Father Rick placed himself in front of the grand piano. It was a beautiful Steinway. The American taxpayers take good care of people in the Witness Protection Program. There was a lot of room around the piano, great space for dancing and for group singing. Father Rick didn't just play hokey wedding music but belted out a string of Gershwin hits. Mom, who is a gifted singer, turned out a lovely rendition of "Summertime," accompanied by Father Rick on the piano. Mom was once the lead singer of her choral group when she was an undergrad at Yale. As Max said, Father Rick is a great piano player, and Mom was the perfect vocalist.

Although our wedding was small, it was perfect. The M&Ms are no longer just an item. Max and I are husband and wife.

Chapter 15

Ifound it easy to adjust to my beautiful apartment in the Witness Protection Program, especially because my roommate is now my husband. My bodyguard, bless him, couldn't be more discreet, occupying his post at a desk in the hallway. I attacked my writing with a newfound excitement. I can't wait to accumulate enough money to give "my girls" something to do, and some extra income to live on.

The title of the latest book I'm working on is *My Favorite Agent*. It was based, of course, on my new life with my favorite FBI agent, Max. We had worked on it quite a bit, especially the love scenes which we "practiced" with live action, wild and wonderful action. My literary agent, Jack Melton, thought the scenes were too "x-rated," so I tuned it down a bit. Just a bit. When I first met Max, I liked him right away. Then, quickly, I fell in love with him, every morsel of him. What I never expected was that Max would become inseparable from the biggest part of my life, my writing. It's as if Max's soul has blended with mine. Working on a book with help from my husband is a gift from heaven.

I asked Max how our waterfront house in Amagansett would fit in with the Witness Protection Program. Max, who swings a lot of clout at the Bureau as well as the Federal Marshalls Service, said he could make it happen. A bit complicated, but given enough disguises, we could head to our vacation house often. There's something about making love with a view of the ocean.

Although a bit strange, our Witness Protection Program lives settled into a routine, a happy routine.

Chapter 16

At noon on a Wednesday afternoon, Max called and said he was bringing over a guy I need to meet.

He walked in with a pleasant-looking man just shy of six feet in height. He was dressed impeccably, I couldn't help but notice. His suit looked like it cost over $5,000. Max introduced him as Trevor McMartin from Adelaide, Australia.

"G'day, mum. My mate here said that his wife is a lovely lady, but I can't help but notice that you are stunningly beautiful. It's a pleasure and honor to meet you."

Charming guy with a charming accent. He's easy to take a liking to. Maybe he can take Max shopping for some new suits.

"Trevor is an amazing guy, Mellie. He's a bank examiner by trade and is probably the best in the world, certainly the best I've ever encountered. He works often with the American government, especially the FBI, and we've been blown away by his talent. Trevor has a way of tracking down money like a fox after prey. It's like he smells the funds and follows the scent. He finds clues that other people would just step over. Trevor is going to help us find what happened to your assets as well as those of the other women authors who've been embezzled. Then he's going to work on getting the money back."

"Twenty million dollars is a sizeable bit of coinage, mum. This is the second largest case I've ever worked on, not counting money stolen directly from governments. I'm happy that my mate here brought me into this."

"I know you've been working on this case for only a week, Trevor, but do you have any leads?" Max said.

"Well, to answer that question, let me ask you folks something. Have you ever heard the name Ali Chudori?"

We both shook our heads.

"He's also known by his American name, or infidel name as he'd call it, Harry Paxton."

Max and I looked at each other, then at Trevor. Then we performed a duet of "holy shit."

I looked at Trevor and said, "He was my quote unquote 'boyfriend' when my money was stolen. I can't believe you've tracked him down."

"Nobody stays hidden from ole Trevor (*Trevah*). "I've only been at this for a week but I'm fair dinkum certain it's him, although I have no idea where he is. Nah worries, Maties, I'll find the bloke. He may be a smart man, but he's never come up against the likes of me. He's left fingerprints all over his terrorist activities. I'll be holed up at FBI headquarters for a few weeks, maybe months. Max, expect to be getting a lot of requests from me for all sorts of information."

"Just ask, Trevor, and we're at your call."

Max had told me this guy Trevor is amazing at what he

does, and he just proved it. From what Max told me about his background, I'm beginning to think of this man as a miracle worker. And he seems confident that he can locate the "bloke." Maybe I'll get my money back and can put my girls to work again.

Trevah, our gift from heaven, heaven *down undah*.

Chapter 17

My latest novel, *The Shadows of Terror*, has just been published by Penguin Random House, and Jack Melton, my literary agent, was freaking out. On the first day, the book hit number one on *The New York Times* Best Seller list. Diligent Jack had managed to get me an advance of $1,000,000. That, combined with the book becoming a sudden best seller, gave me confidence to begin paying my girls. I contacted them and they were happy as hell. The author, as listed on the cover, was me, Melanie Pierce. Some heavies at the FBI asked me to change my name, after Max and I married, to Melanie Wakefield. I flatly refused. In the future, some of my books will be published under my pen name, Michael Hawkins, but formally changing my name would be a lousy idea, given that I became famous (and rich) under the name Melanie Pierce. Can you imagine Danielle Steel changing her name? Max agreed wholeheartedly, God bless him. Not only had my name become a well-known brand, it would be a bad idea to change my name to Wakefield for security reasons. So, Melanie Pierce published yet another book with some heavy denunciations of radical Islam. The book was about the latest new activities of the terrorists, who had decided to go underground and become known by their

"Infidel" names, such as the embezzler Harry Paxton, which is the western name of my former boyfriend and lowlife scumbag, Ali Chudori. One of the characters in the book was "inspired" by that prick.

This was the first book that Max helped me with from cover to cover, working closely with me on the on the sexy parts, very closely. Thanks to the real-life input from my favorite editor, those scenes were wildly popular, according to the many five-star reviews. One reviewer, a *New York Times* best-selling author, wrote: "This book begs you to turn the pages. Not only is it an exciting thriller, but the love scenes are tantalizing and amazing."

That's how I think of Max—tantalizing and amazing. Who would think that sex with my gorgeous husband could result in literary success? Of course, Max's name will never appear in my books. I can never help but notice that women fall all over themselves when looking at Max. I didn't want them to get any ideas from seeing his name in print in a sexy novel. His lovely body is mine, all mine, as well as the rest of him.

Max was concerned, as I was, that my criticism of Islamic radicalism would put me in danger, even though I was in the Witness Protection Program. Just as my research for my books told me, the radical Islamists won't stop until they're achieved their goal, and their goal for authors is scary. Their simple goal is to silence us authors. I had just been assigned a second bodyguard, which did nothing for my nerves. My bodyguards, not to mention my brave pistol-packing husband, made me feel somewhat secure.

Somewhat.

Chapter 18

Diana Blake, popularly known as Dee Blake, is First Lady of the United States. Dee is well-known for her administrative abilities and her keen sense of political strategy. As if she wasn't busy enough, she had recently turned her attention to writing fiction. Her second book, *The Long Journey*, became an overnight best-seller. I may be critical of terrorists in my books, but Dee rips the shit out of them. It probably has a lot to do with the stuff she sees as the right hand of her husband, Matt Blake, President of the United States. I've known Dee for a while, and I really like her. I think of her as a friend and I believe she thinks the same of me. Although I would never tell anybody, the reason I like her has nothing to do with her literary talent, of which she has little. Her writing really sucks. But her famous name rings a bell, and that helps to sell books. Oddly, her poorly written books actually help my sales. It sounds crazy, but my agent has a theory that a lousy book that sells a lot helps the sales of really talented authors, of which, I humbly admit, I'm one. No doubt about it, publishing fiction is a weird business.

But I'm worried about Dee. Max tells me he's heard that the First Lady has been acting strange recently. FBI agents have a way of learning things that aren't publicized, but Max and I share everything with each other, unless I don't have the critical "need to know." I decided to give Dee a call to catch up with her and congratulate her on the sales of her most recent piece of crap. The White House people know me, and usually my calls get through. I must admit that I've become quite famous over the years. The person who picked up the phone sounded hesitant to put me through to the First Lady. What's that about? I wondered. When Dee answered the phone, she sounded different.

"Hi Dee. I just want to congratulate you on *The Long Journey* having made the best seller list. You're carving out a nice second career for yourself when your husband steps down."

"Steps down? Where is he going?"

"You know, when he finishes his term."

"Term? Is he sick?"

My gut told me it was time to shift gears.

"I just finished reading *The Long Journey* and I loved it," I politely lied.

"What journey? Am I going somewhere?"

Every question I asked her resulted in a bizarre response. This conversation was going nowhere, so I figured I'd end it without getting myself any more upset. I've known Dee Blake for a long time, and what I just heard did not sound anything like her.

"Nice talking to you Dee. We'll talk again soon."

"Nice talking to you too. Who did you say you are?"

Holy shit. Could it be that the First Lady of the United States has been whacked with that syndrome, the *Veritas*, the one that other authors have come down with? She definitely sounded like a person with dementia.

I told Max about my strange conversation with Dee Blake.

"Please, honey, not a word to anybody about this. The White House is trying to keep it under wraps."

"Of course, I won't. You know me."

"Yes, I do know you. That's why I love you."

Chapter 19

anice Maloney walked up to the microphone at the Shrine Auditorium in Los Angeles for the American Book Awards event. She was a recent winner of the Pulitzer Prize for fiction for her book, *The Arabian Factor.* *The New York Times* dubbed her, a "Bright New Light on the American Literary Scene." Janice was known for her keen intelligence as well as her skillful way with words. A tall, stunning beauty at six feet, she easily captivated any audience. She was often called to give a talk because of her encyclopedic knowledge and her excellent public speaking skills. She was the keynote speaker at this event, and the crowd of 3,000 gave her a standing ovation when she took her place on the podium.

She was introduced by Wallace Remington, President of the American Book Awards and chairman of the event.

"Ladies and gentlemen," Remington began, "it's my privilege and honor to introduce you to one of the true stars of American literature, a woman of amazing intelligence and keen literary sense. Listen to her and learn from her. Let's hear it for Janice Maloney..."

The crowd cheered for five minutes.

"Thanks, Willy, for your nice words."

Willy? Nobody ever recalled Wallace Remington being referred to as Willy. Remington put a hand to his face to mask his confusion.

"I don't have much to say, so I'll keep this short." She was scheduled to speak for 45 minutes.

"There's been a lot of weird shit going on, and I'm not sure what the fuck I'm supposed to say about it."

The room went silent. Everyone in the audience had a sudden urge to stare at their programs. A few checked their cell phones for messages. Remington took deep breaths to prevent himself from throwing up. To say that the evening became suddenly uncomfortable would be an understatement.

"I have in front of me a bunch of notes, but for some reason I can't read the goddam things. I'm really tired. I think I'll get the fuck out of here."

She walked to the back of the platform but couldn't figure a way to open the curtain. The crowd watched as she jerked the curtain back and forth. Some averted their eyes.

Wallace Remington helped her find an opening in the curtain, and then he walked to the microphone, trying to think of something lighthearted to say. He couldn't come up with anything, so he just introduced the next speaker.

That afternoon, Janice Maloney was admitted to Los Angeles Community Hospital with a diagnosis of early onset dementia. She was 41 years old.

Chapter 20

Max walked into CIA Headquarters in Langley, Virginia, for a meeting with Charles Atkins, Director of the Central Intelligence Agency. He is also known as Gamal Akhbar, but everybody refers to Director Atkins by his popular nickname, Buster. The *Silent Author Case*, as it came to be known, had become a joint effort of the CIA and FBI, with Max heading up the efforts at the FBI. The CIA became involved because a number of cases involved other countries. The alarms were going off as woman after woman had her assets stolen and underwent a drugging that resulted in early onset dementia. The recent fiasco of the famous author, Janice Maloney, where she had a mental breakdown in front of a convention of 3,000, made headlines. Also, the sudden mental illness of the First Lady of the United States put the FBI on full alert, although so far it had been kept from the press.

Buster is a tall, good-looking man of obvious Middle Eastern background, his parents having immigrated from Egypt. Buster speaks fluent Arabic. He's a Coptic Christian, and is well known for his ongoing war with radical Islam. "I'm a jihadi's worst nightmare," Buster would say. "I look like them and I talk like

them, but I'm not one of them. I hunt them down and kill them."
Unlike most CIA Directors, Buster came up through the ranks
as a spy. His predecessor referred to Buster as a "super spook."
Buster is well known as a man who, as he puts it, "takes no shit."
He and Max were old friends, and Max was delighted that they'd
be working a case together. Buster often works directly on cases
as if he were still a field agent.

"These bastards are trying to shut down a significant part of
American literature with their war on authors who have anything
negative to say about Islam in their books," Buster said. "Max, I
know that your charming wife is a potential target, which is why
you had the smarts to put her in the Witness Protection Program.
I've read a few of her books, and wow, she's a fabulous writer,
just the kind of author the radicals are looking to silence. My
wife loves her books too. Bring me up to date on her case."

"She was dating a man who posed as an 'investment counselor'
and took over the management of all of Melanie's financial
affairs. The son of a bitch obtained all her usernames, account
numbers, and passwords, and in one day wiped her out of $20
million dollars. Our old friend, Trevor McMartin from Australia,
found out that Melanie's former 'boyfriend' is an Islamic radical
who goes by the Muslim name of Ali Chudori. The bastard's
American name is Harry Paxton. Nothing gets by Trevor. So,
Melanie's ex-boyfriend has vanished, along with Melanie's assets.
Trevor has him in his crosshairs."

"The worst part is that they are drugging the women, turning
them into demented zombies. Your heads-up spies at the FBI
discovered that the radicals call the stuff *Veritas.* Thank God you
got Melanie into the WPP. From what you've told us, there are
10 women who fit the terrorist's aims, and two of them have been
hit, both financially and physically. What can you tell me about
other women authors?"

"We're arranging to get them all into the Witness Protection Program," Max said, "but I'm looking at the WPP as only a short-term solution. Shit, we can't put every woman author who has negative things to say about Islam into seclusion. And that's only part of the problem. A lot of male authors have written negatively about radical Islam. I have a team at the FBI tallying up the numbers by reading the books. They've come up with 30 other women authors for a total of 40, and 64 men who are also likely targets because of what they write. But for now, they seem to be interested only in women authors. And we're only talking about Americans. Buster, this problem is gigantic."

"Max, you and I have worked many a tough case together. We'll handle this shit. Just take good care of your lovely Melanie. You owe it to her as well as the readers and writers of America."

Chapter 21

Madeline Cranston, age 39, had just published her most recent best seller, *The Days of Winter* through Riordan Publishing Company. The book was about a takeover of a group of small publishers by radical Islamists. Her husband, George, is an oncologist. Just like her good friend, Melanie Pierce, Madeline loved to work with her husband on her books. Like Melanie's husband, Max, George is an enthusiastic fan of his wife's work and enjoyed collaborating with her. They would often have dinner with Max and Melanie, before Melanie became a guest of the Witness Protection Program.

George walked into their Riverdale home at 6:30 p.m., his usual time for arrival. They owned a large house overlooking the Hudson River. Madeline's desk provided a view of the river. Like her friend, Melanie Pierce, she preferred to write in front of an interesting a view.

"Hey, Maddie," he yelled into the den, "I bought some nice champagne. Let's celebrate by toasting *The Days of Winter*. According to *The New York Times*, the book is taking off like a rocket. Hey, honey, where are you?"

Almost like clockwork, Madeline would be sitting in the den catching up on the news when George came home. But she wasn't there. He walked from room to room, calling her name. When he walked into their bedroom, Madeline was sitting on the floor next to the bed with her knees tucked up under her chin.

"Hi, honey, why are you on the floor?"

"Who the hell are you and what the fuck are you doing in my bedroom?"

George called his friend and neighbor, Henry Waxman, a psychiatrist.

Later that evening Madeline Cranston would be admitted to Columbia Presbyterian Hospital with a preliminary diagnosis of early onset dementia.

George didn't bother to put the champagne on ice.

———

Max walked into my Witness Protection Program apartment, having just flown in from his visit to the CIA in Langley, Virginia. I greeted him at the door, and we hugged. I immediately noticed a frown on his face. That's unusual for my smiley husband.

"Mellie, have you heard about your friend Madeline Cranston?"

"Oh shit, she just had a book published, but from the look on your face I don't think that's what you're talking about."

"No, Mellie, I'm not talking about her book. She's the latest victim of that goddam drug that causes dementia, the stuff called *Veritas*. She's in the hospital now. Her husband called the Bureau and told us about it. Honey, this shit is getting out of hand."

"And it's getting worse, Max. Today on TV the CEO of Conklin Publishing Company announced that they will no longer publish a book that contains any criticism of Islam. Did you catch what I just said? I mean if this shit continues, consider the game over, case closed, the scumbags win. If other publishing honchos take that position, the radical Islamists will have achieved their goal, to muzzle the voices of any writer who dares to criticize the bastards. I'm going to double up on my scenes that are critical of radical Islam. Nobody is going to shut *me* up. What do you think, Max?"

"I think I just discovered another reason why I love you. Besides being a fantastic writer, you're a hell of a brave woman and a great American. I agree 100 percent. Nobody is going to shut you up. You're right, honey, this is exactly what the radicals are after, to get the publishing industry to censor itself. That's not the America that you or I know."

"Has the FBI found out anything about that drug they're using on the authors?"

"No, but it's just a matter of time. Nobody has found the drug in its native form. Eventually we will. Then, pray to God, maybe we can find an antidote for it, a cure."

"Let's eat, Max, and then I want to show you what I've written today. I want your opinion."

"The best part of my day is reading your latest words. I love to read your work. Probably has something to do with the fact that I love you."

"You say the sweetest things, honey. Give me a hug."

"After I read your work, I'll give you a lot more than a hug."

"I'm going to hold you to that, you sexy man. I love to screw my favorite editor."

Chapter 22

I had just finished my morning run around the track on the roof of my Witness Protection Program apartment. As usual it felt good to give my lungs their workout. Nothing like a good run to clear your mind. I felt good, but at the same time I felt weird. I felt confused. The place looked different to me. But how the hell can it look different? Don't I live here? The place was familiar, but at the same time it looked strange. Some guy was sitting at the table by what appeared to be an outdoor eating area. Who the hell is he and what's he doing here? I figured I'd ask him.

"Hi," I said. "Who are you?"

He looked at me like I had two heads.

"I'm Tony Forcelli, Melanie. Don't you recognize me?"

"No, I don't. What are you doing here and why did you call me Muldany?"

"I called you Melanie, your name. I'm your FBI bodyguard. Are you feeling okay?"

At 11:30 a.m., I stood by Mellie's bed at Columbia Presbyterian Hospital. I had two other FBI agents with me. I was trying to keep it together, but it was barely working. I felt like my life had just been turned upside down. That's because it had. A man walked in wearing a name badge that identified him as Dr. John Peterson, the chief psychiatrist at the hospital. The head nurse told me that Peterson is Mellie's attending physician. He seemed like a friendly, outgoing guy. He put out his hand for a shake.

"I understand that you're Agent Max Wakefield of the FBI, and this young lady is your wife. Is that correct? I'd like to speak to you alone if that's okay by you."

The other agents nodded and left, positioning themselves outside the door.

"I'm afraid I have some startling news for you, Agent Wakefield."

"Please call me Max. What can you tell me about Melanie?" I think I knew the answer and I felt my legs going weak under me.

"Max, I'm afraid your wife has been inflicted with that drug that causes symptoms of classic early onset dementia. A couple of weeks ago, another woman, age 36, was admitted here with the same symptoms. She's an author, a best seller like your wife. Her name is Rachel Cummings. Another author, Dolores Hartman was also inflicted and is at NYU Langone Hospital. And then there's the well-publicized matter of the novelist Janice Maloney, who had a mental breakdown while addressing a convention. I've read quite a bit about this, Max. Women authors are being given a drug that causes the symptoms of dementia. We think the drug is called *Veritas*. The American Psychiatric Association has asked me to take charge of these cases because of my background in dealing with dementia, including Alzheimer's disease. I've written a book on the subject. Max, we're at the early stages of this goddam mess, and I don't want to give you reasons for false optimism. Right now, we're at the study stage, trying to figure out what we're dealing with. I believe the FBI is involved, am I right?"

"Yes, the FBI is involved and I'm the agent in charge of this case, or should I say cases. It was one of our spies who found out the name of the drug, as you said, *Veritas*."

"Well, in that case, Max, I'll consider you my boss. I promise you I'll do everything in my power to handle this outrage. Can you give me any information that you're free to share?"

"Yes, from what we've put together so far, all of the authors who have been affected have written in their novels a not-so-veiled criticism of radical Islam. We're looking at that as a working hypothesis. If we're correct, someone or more likely some group is behind this, trying to silence my wife and other authors." *And after what they did to Mellie, I intend to leave a few fucking dead bodies behind my investigation,* although I didn't share that thought with Doctor Peterson.

"I'll let you be alone with your wife, Max. I promise you that I intend to see her take her usual place on the best seller list. Consider me your right hand. Be well, my friend."

I felt confident to be working with Dr. Peterson. I had heard a lot about him, and he seemed to fit the bill with his reputation. He's a good guy, an expert in his field, and most important, he gives a shit about his patients.

I leaned over and stroked Mellie's face. I was happy as hell that she smiled at me. She actually seemed to recognize me, which I took as a good sign. "Can I give you a kiss, honey?"

My happiness didn't last for long.

"Of course, you can give me a kiss, Daddy. You're my father."

Chapter 23

I got a call from Walter Townsend, the director of the FBI scientific research department. I invited him over to have dinner with Melanie and me, but now, of course, it was just me. My Mellie is in the psychiatric ward of Columbia Presbyterian Hospital, and I feel like I'm about to lose my mind too.

"You look concerned about something, Walter." I said.

"One of the guards at your old apartment became concerned when a guy showed up supposedly to deliver a case of bottled water. He had no appointment, nor was the guard alerted that he was coming. When questioned, the deliveryman said it was given to him by a person he didn't know. The guard cuffed him and placed him under arrest. With his heads-up thinking, the guard ordered the case of water to be taken to the FBI lab. When they did some testing, they noticed a strange substance in all the water. They tested it on rodents and the animals went into brain space. All of the lab rats showed animal symptoms similar to dementia. The reason for my sourpuss was my realization that the water was meant for Melanie. Apparently, this wasn't the first illegal delivery made to your apartment, and my thinking is that Melanie had ingested something from a previous drop off. My heart goes out to you, Max. Melanie has obviously taken the drug and we're guessing that it was in some liquid in your place. Thank God you didn't drink any. That's the bad news, but it's accompanied by some good news. Thanks to your wife's bodyguard, we believe we have our hands on the substance that's been raising hell with those women. It's undergoing rigorous testing now."

Rigorous testing? It can't be too rigorous for me. Mellie, my Mellie, the most important part of my life, now has the mind of an Alzheimer's victim. I thought my heart would crack in two when she referred to me as Daddy. This testing can't be rigorous enough, or fast enough.

Chapter 24

I had lunch with my cousin Sheila Jackson, Mellie's best friend, her BFF as she calls her. I've pulled out all stops with my investigation, especially since Mellie was stricken with that goddam *Veritas* drug. I've met with Sheila many times before, and we usually catch up with each other on the phone once a week. With her sharp brain, she'd make a damn good detective. She has a handle on scientific subjects that I find awesome. Besides being cousins, we're also good friends. Sheila was responsible for Mellie and me getting together, and that puts her at the top of my good friends list. I was impressed not only with her strong friendship with Mellie, but also for her sharp as hell intelligence. She edits complex scientific works, and her brilliant mind is just what I need to help get my investigation done. Maybe Sheila can help lead me in a direction I hadn't gone before.

Sheila had just come back from the hospital where she visited Mellie. She cried when she described her visit. Mellie had no idea who she was, and that tore at Sheila's insides. She's been Mellie's best friend for years, ever since college, and Sheila told me she felt like she lost a sister. When I told her that Mellie thought I was her father, she sobbed out loud. I had visited her the first thing this morning and there was no change. Mellie still calls me "Daddy."

We spoke with no agenda. When I search for clues, I always go wide, not wanting any preconceived notions to throw me off. We discussed the whole issue of dementia and people we've known who were stricken with it, mainly elderly relatives. She talked about her grandmother, age 89, and her current status as a resident of a nursing home.

"Until four years ago, Grandma was sharp as a tack and funny as hell. Then we began to lose her as she started to forget small things. Within a couple of months Grandma was nobody, a person who looked familiar but who we didn't know anymore. It's incredibly sad, the worst kind of illness I can imagine. Death is one thing, but when a person's entire personality disappears it's almost as final as death, but in a way it's even worse because you can see the person's body, but the mind has fled. But seeing it inflicted on young people is pure horror. Seeing Mellie like that tears me apart as I know it does you, Max."

"Yes, it's accurate to say it tears me apart."

"The killer is that she, as well as her fellow authors are so young, so goddam young," Sheila said. "It almost reminds me of that weird case a few years ago that law enforcement people called '*The Scent of Revenge.*' Young prominent women were sprayed in the face with a substance that inflicted them with early onset dementia. Mel even discussed *The Scent of Revenge* in a couple of her books. She thought it was a great story angle to work into her thrillers. She doesn't miss a trick. Thank God they found a cure."

Holy shit, where the hell has my head been? Sheila just mentioned the case that we should have looked at from the beginning. Sometimes I get so wrapped up in my work that I overlook the obvious. I've read every one of Mellie's books twice, and I missed the connection. I fucking missed it.

"Sheila, you just hit the ball out of the park. Of course, *The Scent of Revenge*, a case amazingly close to what we're looking at. I'm trying to remember the detective who honchoed that case."

"Bennie Weinberg," Sheila said, "aka Bennie-the-Bullshit Detector. As I'm sure you know, he's a detective with the NYPD and he's also a board-certified psychiatrist. He even wrote a book about the case entitled, appropriately enough, *The Scent of Revenge*. I was the editor of his final draft, and I can tell you he's one sharp cookie. You should try to get in touch with him, Max. He may lead you in some interesting directions."

"Sheila, I'm thinking of trying to recruit you into the FBI. You're brilliant, cuz. You've just opened a door that I didn't even know was there."

Chapter 25

I sat with my sister, Debbie Wakefield, in her office at One Police Plaza. She's a Detective First Grade with the New York Police Department. My "little" sister is age 32, two years younger than me. She's tall at 6'1," and pretty. Debbie is also sweet and polite, decidedly feminine. She never thinks about putting on a macho "tough cop" persona, relying instead on her considerable brain power to do her job. Debbie's single, and our cousin Sheila and I have been on the lookout for a suitable guy for her.

This morning we visited Mellie in the hospital. Mellie still calls me "Daddy" and referred to Debbie as "Mom." Debbie, who seldom cries, broke down in tears at the sight of her sister-in-law. Mr. Tough Guy joined her.

Debbie is friends with Bennie Weinberg, the detective-psychiatrist, and has worked many a case with him. Debbie seems to know instinctively that collaborating with intelligent colleagues is a great way to get a job done. I recalled meeting Bennie a couple of years before, but never got to know him well, although I knew all about his reputation as a whiz. Debbie thinks he's the smartest person in the NYPD, and she never exaggerates.

We agreed that it would be a good idea for me to meet first with Bennie alone.

When I walked into his office, Bennie almost jumped out of his chair to greet me. He's a friendly, gregarious guy, even though his job involves a lot of gruesome mayhem. He's about 5'10, slightly bald, and a bit overweight, which he makes up for by wearing expensive designer suits. My sister admires the fact that he doesn't try to hide his encroaching baldness with a comb over.

Bennie's nickname is Bennie-the-Bullshit-Detector, a label he wears because of his uncanny talent for spotting lies, especially on the witness stand. He's a hit with prosecutors, who say that having Bennie observe a witness is like having a polygraph in the courtroom. Bennie is a graduate of Harvard Medical School, and, as you might expect, he's smart as hell, even though he speaks with the street mouth of a hardened cop. He's also a good detective, serving the NYPD as a Detective First Grade.

"I'm really sorry to hear about that charming and lovely wife of yours, Max. I understand that she's been hospitalized."

"Yes, she's apparently been infused with that *Veritas* shit. Bennie, I'm embarrassed to say this but my sister Debbie, as well as my cousin Sheila, both think that the rash of women authors who've been administered the dementia-causing drug, reminds them of that *Scent of Revenge* case you worked on a few years ago. I say I'm embarrassed, because, as an FBI agent, I should have spotted the similarities myself from the get-go. If I recall, a group of jihadis were going around spraying a substance into the faces of prominent women. I say prominent, because all of them were well-known, and they all had one thing in common, a criticism of radical Islam. How am I doing so far?"

"You've done your homework, Max. In working that *Scent of Revenge* case, we discovered a jihadi honcho named Dmitri

Pushkin, known among his colleagues as 'the chemist.' He was the bastard who invented that stuff known as the *Scent of Revenge*. Pushkin was killed in a shoot-out, but we discovered his research papers when we raided the factory where they manufactured the shit in Baltimore. The drug caused symptoms of severe dementia. You couldn't tell the difference between an Alzheimer's patient and someone who was hit with the Scent of Revenge. From Pushkin's papers, we found the formula they used to make the substance. Using reverse engineering, we soon came upon a drug we could use to counter the effects of The Scent. As fate would have it, the cure is a widely used drug to treat the flu. It's known as Tralforlalazine. Say that three times fast. It may be a tongue twister, but it gave us the weapon to fight the *Scent of Revenge*. It's relatively harmless and its only known side-effects are joint pain, which usually subsides within a couple of weeks."

"You know my next question, Bennie. Do you think this Tralforlalazine stuff can be used for *Veritas*, the dementia-causing drug the authors have been hit with?"

I took a deep breath, not sure if I wanted him to say yes or no.

"All I can give you, Max, is an educated guess. Because the stuff is harmless, may I suggest that we try it on your lovely wife? As I said, Tralforlalazine is innocuous with mild and short-term side effects. I wouldn't make this recommendation if I didn't think it was safe."

Bennie put me on the spot, and it was a spot where I belonged. I was the person who needed to make the big decision. When I first met Mellie, I liked her a lot. It was impossible not to, even though I met her for a criminal investigation. She had a warmth about her that was undeniable. Also, she had a hilarious sense of humor. The fact that she was the most beautiful woman I had ever seen helped with my growing affection for her. I think she liked me too. Well, it was obvious that she did. I've read about

93

the kind of love we have in novels, mainly Mellie's books. But our love isn't fiction, it's a beautiful reality. Our early affection turned to love, a deep love that consumed me. I wasn't rushing anything when I asked her to marry me. It was simply an obvious direction my life had taken, a life with Mellie. But now she has dementia and thinks and acts like it. The past few weeks seem like a lifetime. That she sees me as her father is the worst form of sadness I could ever imagine. As an FBI agent, I've learned to control my emotions. It's an important part of the job. But my emotions were anything but under control. I've got to get her back, her love, her brilliance, her fun—my life.

I took a deep breath. The idea of trying a drug on Mellie tore at my insides, but if there's anyone I can trust it's Bennie Weinberg. Hell, he's an MD, not just a cop. And he cares, an obvious fact you could tell by looking at his face. If we can stop Mellie from thinking I'm her father, it's worth a try.

"Bennie, let's do it."

Chapter 26

That afternoon, Bennie and I walked into Columbia Presbyterian Hospital. Bennie had spent an hour with Dr. John Peterson, Mellie's attending physician, the doctor in charge of the medical investigation into the dementia-causing drug. Bennie brought Peterson up to date on the amazing drug, Tralforlalazine. Dr. Peterson accompanied us to Mellie's room.

Over the years I've grown accustomed to danger. In Afghanistan a was almost killed, a bullet missing my head by inches. Also, life in the FBI can get scary at times. But those fears were nothing like I felt as we entered Mellie's room. I was scared shitless.

Mellie was awake. She looked as beautiful as ever, but she also looked confused, which did nothing for my broken heart. I gently held her hand as I leaned over and kissed her.

"Hi, Daddy, nice to see you."

I looked at Bennie, who respectfully closed his eyes. Then I glanced at Dr. Peterson, who did the same.

"Mellie, this is my friend Bennie. He's here to say hello to you."

"Hi Lennie," she said, having missed his name. "Somebody took the hair off the top of your head."

"Nice to meet you, Melanie. It's called baldness," Bennie said with a chuckle.

We chatted for a few minutes making small talk. With Mellie, the only talk is small talk. Mellie, the smartest person I've ever met, the most brilliant novelist in the country if not the world, now babbles like an infant.

Bennie leaned over and sprayed a small cloud of Tralforlalazine into Mellie's face. He had told me that she would probably doze off and that it would take a few minutes to have its effect. I looked at my watch for the umpteenth time since he sprayed her with the stuff. Five minutes had gone by.

She took a deep breath and blinked her eyes. She looked at me and smiled.

"Hi, Daddy. Who's your friend?"

Mr. Tough Guy FBI Agent broke down and sobbed. The Tralforlalazine obviously didn't work. I was hoping for a miracle, but Mellie still thinks I'm her "Daddy." I'd been disappointed in my life, but nothing like this. I imagine this is how Mellie felt when, early in her writing career, she got a rejection letter.

Now what?

Chapter 27

Bennie, Dr. John, and I met in a small office near Mellie's room. I guessed that I looked like a broken-down vagrant.

"Hey, Max," Bennie said. "I'm not here to play Dr. Feelgood, I'm here to be Dr. Reality. I know you're devastated by what we just saw, but I want you to snap out of it. What just happened can be labelled a disappointment, nothing more than that. We had hope, and I emphasize the word hope, that the Tralforlalazine would work with that *Veritas* substance just like it worked with the *Scent of Revenge*. Didn't happen, but that doesn't mean shit. We came up with Tralforlalazine when we reverse engineered The Scent. And it worked. We haven't done that yet with the drug in question. All we did was administer the drug we knew. I am totally fucking confident that we can find a cure for this syndrome just like we did for the *Scent of Revenge* after scientific testing and reverse engineering. Dr. John, what are your thoughts?"

"I absolutely agree with Bennie," Peterson said. "It will take some time, but let science show the way. We know we have the substance that causes the syndrome. Now the technicians just need to work the hell out of it. I'd feel positive if I were you,

Max. Bennie's right. What just happened was a disappointment, nothing more serious than that."

I felt better. I knew these two weren't just spouting positive thinking bullshit to cheer me up, they were talking science. Time for me to put my rational-thinking hat on. There's a way out of this shit, but we just haven't found that way yet. I need to stop looking at Mellie through the eyes of a man with a broken heart. She needs me to be there for her, to give her whatever strength I have. And the way for me to do that isn't by acting like a fucking idiot when she calls me "Daddy." I've always thought of myself as a tough guy. I showed it when I was awarded all those decorations for serving in Afghanistan, and I've shown it through countless FBI investigations. Mellie needs me to be tough like I've been trained, not a weeping candyass.

After our meeting, I immediately returned to the FBI field office and went straight to the lab. I've been an FBI agent long enough to know how to get results, which was exactly what I intended to do with the lab technicians. Of course, getting results sometimes means acting diplomatically, which is what I did. I spoke to Frank Meyers, the head of the lab. I showed him photos of Mellie, before and after she came down with the syndrome. I also showed him one of her marketing brochures which touted her fabulous best-selling books. I filled him in on our relationship and told him how much I loved her. I could see this guy was a solid human being, and I think I got to him— big time.

"Max, I'm not going to bullshit you. This case is my highest priority, even more so after what you've just told me. So, here's a promise, my friend. I'm going to lead the effort to come up with an antidote for that syndrome. You can take that to the bank. Call me everyday or stop by and I'll give you constant updates on where we're going. All I request is a signed copy of

Melanie's next best seller, which I fully intend that she'll write very soon."

Chapter 28

It's been two weeks since Mellie came down with the syndrome, two weeks of testing at the FBI lab. I visit Mellie twice a day and bite my lip as she calls me "Daddy." I've always been a big believer in science, but seeing my brilliant wife acting like an Alzheimer's victim puts my brain on hold and tears me apart. Two weeks isn't long in the ways of scientific investigation, but to me it felt like a lifetime. I trust Frank Meyers, the lab director. I've become friends with him, and I know he's doing his best to come up with a solution, an antidote, a cure. But "doing his best" takes time. I know that. I just wish that my stomach could accept that. This case is a lot tougher than that *Scent of Revenge* matter. In that case they were lucky to find an antidote in a commonly used drug right off the shelf, Tralforlalazine. But, as we found out, it doesn't work with the drug the authors have been hit with, *Veritas*. They're going to need to design a new drug. Once they do, the answer can come in one of two ways: A commonly used drug, or a drug that may consist of combining substances that will require approval of the Food and Drug Administration, a process that can take months if not years. No way would any of my colleagues in the FBI be willing to go against the FDA rules.

I just got the call I've been waiting for. Frank Myers from the FBI lab thinks they've found the antidote, as sure as they can be without actual human testing. It's a combination of off-the-shelf ingredients, but because it's a combination resulting in a new drug, it needs FDA approval.

FDA approval? Holy shit, that can take forever. I called none other than Sarah Watson, Director of the FBI, my boss. Sarah's also an old friend. She's quite fond of Mellie and is willing to go out of her way to help. She's familiar with the *Silent Author Case* as if it's the back of her hand. Sarah, God bless her, called the Director of the FDA, a man she knew quite well. With her brilliant skills of diplomacy, not to mention her considerable power, she convinced the FDA to fast track the approval process. Instead of taking months or years, the drug was approved within a week, especially because the ingredients are harmless. God bless Sarah Watson! She's right up there at the top of my list of favorite people. Then I spoke to Dr. John Peterson, Mellie's attending physician. I also spoke to Bennie Weinberg. I gave them both the good news.

Bennie and I met Dr. Peterson in Mellie's room, along with Frank Myers, the lab head. I asked my good friend, Father Rick Sampson, to be there as well because I needed spiritual support. Father Rick led us in prayer. Dr. Peterson then gave Mellie the drug in tablet form. She was awake, and happy to see her "Daddy" at her bedside. After our prayer, I remained on my knees. Frank Myers said it should take five minutes to have its effect, the longest five minutes of my life. Mellie awoke after dozing. I stood and moved next to her bed.

She looked at me, smiled, reached out and grabbed my hand.

"Hi, Max honey. What are these folks doing here? Am I in a

hospital for something?"

"Max, you called me Max."

"Well that's your friggin name, bozo." Along with her awareness, Mellie's wiseass sense of humor was back.

"Melanie," Dr. Peterson said, "Is it okay if I ask you a dumb question? Can you identify this man to my right?"

"Of course, he's my husband, Max Wakefield. He's an FBI agent. I'm sorry but I don't recognize the rest of you folks."

I held her face in both my hands. "Oh, my God, Mellie. You're back with us."

"That's nice," she said, looking confused but smiling, "but where the hell have I been?"

With everybody looking on, I explained to her exactly what happened during the past two weeks.

"So, I was hit with that same shit the other women authors were whacked with? I can't believe that it's been two goddam weeks. The last thing I remember was standing next to our rooftop track having just finished my morning run. I remember a guy who said he was my bodyguard looking worried. The next thing I remember was waking up here with you and these guys. Max, honey, you look like a wreck. How about a hug?"

Bennie, Dr. Peterson, Frank, and Father Rick all had tears in their eyes. I guessed my ranting and raving over the past couple of weeks had gotten to them. This was the happiest reunion I could ever imagine.

Dr. Peterson took care of checking Mellie out of the hospital. I wanted to invite the guys back to our place for lunch, but the Witness Protection Program doesn't allow for visitors. No problem. They all seemed to understand that Mellie and I needed to be alone together. My Mellie was back. My life was back.

Chapter 29

I've had some weird shit happen to me in my life, but this tops it all. For two weeks, I was in space. But now I'm back on earth, back with my man, back with my girls, back with Mom. Max and I sat on the couch in the living room overlooking Central Park. He had his arm around me, and my head was on his shoulder. He still looked like a wreck. I had one purpose, to cheer Max up, to bring my wonderful husband back to his old positive self. From my perspective, I simply slept for two weeks, not remembering anything. Max, on the other hand, thought he had lost me, our relationship, our life together, our love. I listened to him tell me about every minute of his life while I was in la-la land. I had nothing to add because I was mercifully out of it. I can't imagine going for two weeks without Max recognizing me. Knowing that he was without me for two weeks made me appreciate my feelings toward him. Oh my God, am I in love— all over again. Listening to him tell me about his two weeks alone was tough, but now we're back together.

"So, I guess you'd prefer that I don't call you Daddy," my wiseass mouth said.

"Don't even think about it, if you don't mind. Watching you in that hospital bed thinking that I was your father broke my heart. I love you baby. I love you more than life itself. It's unbelievably wonderful to have you back, back in my arms. Hey, I feel like a mess after waiting to see you react to that drug, sweating like a racehorse all the while. I want to take a quick shower."

"Want company?"

"Yes. Oh dear Lord, yes."

"Got anything in mind after our shower?"

"Yes, let's make love like we've never done it before. Let's make love like we're reinventing it."

"You're on, honey. I can't wait to feel you inside me—It's where you belong, baby."

The M&Ms are back on the block.

Chapter 30

Not all cases have a positive conclusion, but at least the *Silent Author Case* had a happy ending—so far. The FBI lab found a cure for the dementia-causing drug, that goddam scourge known as *Veritas*. After I was administered the antidote, they gave it to the other women authors who had been affected. They all responded, just like I had, thank God. Like I said, it was a happy ending, or at least it seemed that way.

I got a call from none other than Matt Blake, President of the United States. He called to congratulate me on being back among the living. He's always the gracious gentleman, one of the reasons I like him, I vote for him, and contribute money to his campaigns. But I don't go public with my fondness for him. Always a bad idea for authors to risk alienating a part of the reading market. Then he put First Lady Dee on the phone.

"Mel, honey, I understand that you phoned me while I was a space cadet. Like you, I'm happy to be back on earth. I don't need to tell you about the subject of your next book, do I? How about something like *Beating Veritas,* or maybe *The Truth about Veritas*? I'll be happy to give you a plug on the back cover. In exchange, maybe you can teach me how to write."

Dee is such a sweetheart, and her humility is inspiring. She knows she's a lousy writer and sells books on the strength of her name alone. But hearing her say it blew me away. I immediately volunteered to be the first reader and editor for her next book, which will be a *BIG JOB*. I liked her idea about writing a novel about my experience with *Veritas*. But my experience with the subject consisted of being semi-conscious. Maybe Max can write it with me.

The *Silent Author Case* is far from over, but at least the disabling drug has been conquered. There's still the question of the missing money, including my $20 million. Needless to say, that part of the case still has my major attention, as well as the focus of Max and the rest of the FBI. Hopefully, Trevor McMartin, our friend from *down undah*, will soon come up with some major clues.

Chapter 31

nough stress. It's time to head to the ocean, to Amagansett. No sense owning a waterfront mansion if you can't use it to chill out. Max and I invited his sister Debbie, along with my good buddy Sheila and her husband, Chuck. Plenty of room for everybody.

The romantic in me kicked into high gear. Both Max and I want to find a guy for Max's sister Debbie. She's tall, beautiful, with a sweet personality, even though she's a cop with the NYPD. My pal Sheila, of course, signed up for our *find Debbie a boyfriend* campaign. Sheila loves her cousin Debbie, and wants her to settle down with a great guy, just like Max and I want her to.

I thought I may know just the man—maybe. I bounced the idea off Max and I also told Sheila, who had met the guy a couple of times. They both loved the idea. He's a man who Max and I befriended on one of our trips here. Jason Milburn is Chief of Police of the Amagansett Police Department, a somewhat quiet job. Not a whole lot of crime happens in our seaside hamlet except for an occasional burglary and a drunk driving arrest. He moved to Amagansett two years ago after his parents left him their vacation home. He lived in Manhattan at the time and served as a detective with the NYPD. Maybe he and Debbie know each other, although I didn't want to spoil the fun by telling them they'd both be at our get-together. Jason is a good-looking guy, not a knockout like my Max, but close. He's 37 years old, six foot three, blond hair, and an athletic build. He's also a nice guy, including his charming *New Yawk* accent.

Max and I sat having drinks on our deck overlooking the ocean along with Sheila, Chuck, and Debbie.

Jason, who lives just a couple of blocks away, came walking up the steps holding a bottle of wine and a beautiful bouquet of daffodils. Like I said, he's a nice guy, and thoughtful too.

When he got to the deck, he and Debbie locked eyes. A few moments went by, a few awkward moments. Then, they yelled each other's name. Yes, they yelled. After they quieted down, they hugged, a bit more than a "long-time-no-see" hug.

Looks like Max and Mellie, the matchmakers, may have hit one over the fence. Obviously, Debbie and Jason knew one another, and they sure seemed happy to be together again.

They stood with their arms around each other, looking cute as hell. They're both tall, he at six three and Debbie at six one. My romantic mind imagined how tall their children would be, and I imagined taking Debbie shopping for clothes for their sprouting kids. Chill, Mellie, let things happen as they want to happen. Jason and Debbie told us about how they worked together, often at the same crime scene. They weren't formal partners, but they acted like they wanted to be. As they spoke, I thought I was listening to a boy and girlfriend shooting the shit over old times. They stared into each other's eyes as they told their story, holding hands all the while.

Max and I walked into the kitchen to get the steaks for the barbecue grill. He winked at me, pinched my butt, and kissed me on the ear. I think Max is in touch with his inner romantic just like I am.

"Hey, wiseguy," Debbie said, playfully slapping Jason's arm, "How come you suddenly left the NYPD? I miss you." She misses him! Yesss.

"I invited you to come out and visit me here, but you were always too busy. I'm happy we finally got together—*really happy*," he said softly. I looked at Debbie's face and thought she'd melt when he said that. Max had told me that his sister is so dedicated to her work that she's always too busy to take time off. Something told me that she just found a way to take her mind off work.

We had a great barbecue party. I noticed that Debbie and Jason couldn't seem to keep their hands off each other. Their eyes constantly locked, causing my romantic heart to flutter. I think I'll write a novel about this experience._

―――――――

The following weekend, Max and I again rented a car and headed out to Amagansett. We really love the place and promised each other we'd visit as often as we could. Max has an amazing talent for negotiating with FBI honchos and the Federal Marshalls Service to get me permission to leave my WPP apartment. We were both disguised and armed, and travelled with an FBI bodyguard. As soon as we arrived, Jason invited us to his house for coffee. Debbie, no surprise, was there. His house was lovely, nowhere near as big as ours, but nicely appointed. Having just gotten out of the pool, Debbie was wearing a yellow bikini, and it looked great on her tall, slim body. Jason couldn't seem to keep his eyes off her. They constantly held hands and stroked each other's arms. No doubt about it, we were in the presence of two happy lovers.

"Debbie and I are hosting a little party here next week, and we'd love to have you guys join us."

"Great," I said, "what's the occasion if I may ask?"

"It's an engagement party. Debbie and I are getting married." They kissed.

Holy shit, I thought I'd pass out, my romantic heart flickering like a sock in the wind. I hugged Max, then I hugged Debbie and Jason.

Max and Mellie, the M&M Matchmakers. Yesss!

Chapter 32

At 10 a.m. on Tuesday morning I was doing research for a novel I'm thinking of writing. Often my research will make the decision for me. Sometimes I come up with a story idea, but after doing research I decide it sucks. It's better to let the idea announce itself. One idea seemed to stick, a novel inspired by the romance between Debbie and Jason. I already started to jot notes for the plot. Watching those two together kicked my romance writer's heart into gear. The phone rang. It was Max.

"Our old friend, Trevor, just buzzed me and says he wants to meet us in my office. He sounded really happy about something. Do you think he's got some interesting news for us?"

"Oh my God. You mean like $20 million dollars' worth of interesting news? I'll be there in a few minutes." My books have been selling well and I've been getting large advances. But the idea of getting back my $20 million suddenly got me excited. I think the reason for my excitement is that I now have a wonderful person to share it with—Max. Hold on. Don't get ahead of myself. We haven't spoken to Trevor yet. But Max said he sounded really happy.

When I walked into Max's office, Trevor (*Trevah*), was sitting in front of his desk wearing what can only be described as a shit eating grin.

"G'day, Mum. Well, Maties, as I told you, ole Trevah would never let you down. I'm happy to say that I've tracked down Melanie's funds and have taken temporary possession of them in the name of the United States government. All $20 million is safely tucked into treasury bills. All I need to know is what name to put on the account so I can transfer the money. I assume it's Melanie Pierce."

I felt like I was going to faint. Trevor found my money! I quickly answered Trevor's question.

"Melanie Pierce and Max Wakefield are the names to put on the funds. Max and I are one entity."

"Mel, honey, are you serious?" Max said.

"Of course, I'm serious. You and I are one." I meant it, of course. Max got up and hugged me. I was happy for another opportunity to show Max how much I love him.

"I also managed to find the current address of the bloke who stole the money. I'm sure Max and his mates will love to pay him a fair dinkum visit with their guns drawn. Unfortunately, his address is in Yemen."

So, I'm loaded again, or I should say, the M&Ms are loaded. Since I'm cured of that *Veritas* drug, I think it's time to move out of the Witness Protection Program. I'm sure Max can clear it with the FBI and the Federal Marshalls Service. This apartment is a great place but it's not ours. We now have enough money to find a place that's *beyond* nice.

Chapter 33

Max and I planned to go apartment shopping the day after we got the wonderful news from Trevor. My old apartment, being large at 1800 square feet, should fetch a nice buck. I bought it four years ago so I should make a good profit because the Manhattan real estate market in an ass-kicking mood. Max still owns a co-op, which would probably sell within a week. My talented literary agent did a great job of negotiating large advances of a million each for my two most recent books. So, my advances, my huge book royalties, the profits from the sale of our apartments, not to mention a reinfusion of $20 million, told us to go for it big time. Really big.

The next day, we both thought we found it, a 3,000 square foot beauty just a couple of blocks from my WPP digs. It was on Fifth Avenue and 66th Street. The view of Central Park was even better than my WPP place, and it was closer to the Central Park Zoo, a place I love to stroll around for inspiration. It had four bedrooms, including a huge *en suite* master with a large bathroom and a hot tub. The kitchen was so decked out I could cook for an army. Just like my WPP place, the apartment came with a huge roof but even bigger than the WPP apartment. The roof included a garden, a running track, and an outdoor entertainment area. Hey, we have a few bucks, more than enough to take care of my girls as well as ourselves. Why not enjoy the money?

We both looked at our broker, and in one voice said, "We'll take it."

The next weekend we would attend Jason and Debbie's engagement party in Amagansett, a party that is largely the result of Max and me—The Matchmakers. Instead of renting a car to drive to Amagansett, we hired a limo. Why not?

I was happy with all the good stuff that was happening. Will it last? Maybe I can write the next chapter of the story myself.

If only.

Chapter 34

Debbie called and told us that Jason had just taken his old job as a detective with the NYPD. We were happy for them, because now they would live together in Manhattan and still be able to visit Jason's vacation house in Amagansett. Max and I looked forward to palling around with them regularly.

Max's sister and Jason reminds me of the time Max and I met. Although we hadn't known each other before, like Debbie and Jason, I was reminded of love at first sight. Well, to be accurate it took a day for us to go from liking each other to being madly in love. Hey, I'm a novelist. Nothing wrong with a little romantic musing, especially when it involves Max.

During our ride back from Amagansett I came up with a story for my next novel. That's the way it happens. Suddenly a story announces itself to my brain, and then it's up to me to fill in the details. Unlike some writers, I don't do a thorough outline before I begin to write. The reason I don't come up with a detailed outline is because I never know the full story when I begin to write, especially the end. Like I read in Stephen King's book, *On Writing*, I just come up with the basic idea and then follow my characters as *they tell me* the story. I just insert my interesting characters into a scene and they take it from there. But this book would be different because I already know all the details. It will be a novel patterned exactly on me and Max. I've included scenes from our lives in past novels, such as *My Favorite Agent*, but this book would be an exact story of our love affair and marriage. I chose different names, of course, and changed the scenery and locations so that nobody would guess the book was about us. We had a wonderful time writing the book, reminding us of how our relationship started slowly and rapidly evolved into our life together. It reminded me of when I first realized I was in love with Max, and how it continues every day of our lives. The main characters are Sam and Samantha. Dumb, I know, but somehow cool. The title of the book will be *A Case of Love*. The word "case" was short for Samantha's criminal case that Sam the detective was investigating. Too adorable? Maybe. I think I'm a better writer than I am a title assigner, but for the time being, that's the title. The final decision is up to my publisher, of course.

I set a shorter deadline than I do for most of my books—one month, which I'm sure will make my girls happy. I felt confident that the book would do well. When you've knocked a few out of the ballpark like I've done, a large readership is almost guaranteed for your next book. Just as when people see Stephen King, J.K. Rowling, or Nelson DeMille, many readers will simply buy the book without even looking for a story synopsis. I'm happy to say that my books are up there with the big boys. Well, I guess I *am* one of the big boys.

After dinner, I grabbed Max by the hand and led him to the bedroom. As the great English novelist Jack London once said, "You can't wait for inspiration, you have to go after it with a club." So, I went after inspiration with a club, making love to my favorite leading character. Max knows how to swing a club too. Wow, does he ever.

Chapter 35

Because so many of the impacted authors were from New York City, including Mellie, NYPD Commissioner Ralph Norquist asked FBI Director Sarah Watson if the NYPD could work the *Silent Author Case* in conjunction with the FBI. Sarah discussed it with me as the lead FBI agent on the case, and I readily agreed, having worked with the NYPD many times before. They have good people, talented detectives like my sister Debbie. Norquist assigned the NYPD files to Debbie, along with the newly rehired detective Jason Milburn, who is now Debbie's husband. I will be still the lead agent on the case. So, the *Silent Author Case* would soon become a family affair, including Mellie, who recently experienced the *Veritas* drug herself.

Director Sarah convened a meeting at her New York Office at 26 Federal Plaza. NYPD Commissioner Ralph Norquist was part of the meeting, along with Debbie, Jason, me, and Mellie. Mellie was invited not only because she actually suffered the result of the terrorist activity, but also because she has the mind of a detective, having written so many crime novels. Actually, Mellie has one of the sharpest detective minds I've ever encountered, and I've been involved with quite a few of them. She studies criminal investigations with the zeal of a university scholar, and her best-selling books show it. I mean, shit, I'm a lot better investigator just from reading Mellie's books.

"We've just received some shocking news from a couple of our undercover spies," Sarah said. "Max, I haven't even told you about it because I just got this information less than an hour ago. As we all know, the FBI lab came up with an antidote to that crap they call *Veritas*. That's why we have Melanie back with us, thank God. Now, from the reports I've just heard, the terrorists may resort to kidnapping of authors. You heard me—kidnapping. Mellanie, I don't want to disrupt your life by asking you to reenter the Witness Protection Program, so I'm assigning a full-time bodyguard to you. He or she will occupy an apartment next to your brownstone. Because of your fabulous writing, Mellanie, we think you're a prime target, as we saw when you were hit with that drug. I know you're licensed to carry a firearm and have a concealed-carry permit. I suggest you carry your weapon any time you leave your house, even though you will have a bodyguard with you. As you know, the jihadis want to silence any criticism of radical Islam, and from our experience we know that they won't give up. Melanie, you told me that you have no intention of censoring herself because of the threats, and I completely agree with you. I say that as a freedom-loving American, not as FBI Director. No way in hell should authors kowtow to the demands of radicals. I admire you for your courage, Melanie, and for your dedication to the First Amendment. Any thoughts, folks? Detective Debbie, I see your hand up."

"I've worked cases with my brother Max before, as well as with my new husband, Jason. I know that I have a reputation as a soft-spoken detective, but I just want to assure you that I can shoot the balls off a gnat at 50 yards. Don't worry, Madam Director, with Max leading the charge we'll handle this case."

I love my sister, Debbie, and she just showed one of the reasons why. Yes, she's soft-spoken but she's tough as nails, a really good cop. I think I've got a great team to work with.

"Okay, folks," Sarah Watson said, "we've got work to do—very dangerous work."

Chapter 36

Sheik Mustaffa Creezin met with his colleague Ali Chudori, aka investment counsellor Harry Paxton, in Paxton's "safe-house" apartment on the Lower East Side of Manhattan, near Greenwich Village.

"Ali, the Infidel scum have achieved a modest success with their antidote to our holy drug, *Veritas*. Typical of the fools, they believe they have defeated us. Nothing could be further from the truth as you well know, brother Ali. Our new plan is to kidnap, *temporarily* kidnap, each and every Infidel bitch who writes words critical of Islam. Each of them will be ordered to carry out our simple objective. They will submit every one of their books to us before publication—every book. If there are any words critical of Islam, our plan of violence will go into effect. Not only will they delete critical words, they will also write chapters in praise of Islam. They will have no choice as it will be explained to them. They can and will go to the authorities, but it will not matter. They will still have no rational choice. The Infidels will soon see a new form of terrorism, *Editorial Terrorism*."

"Brother Creezin, it is no wonder why we call you 'Sheik,' that word of honor. You are brilliant in the works of Allah."

"Brother Ali, *Veritas* still exists. But now it isn't in the form of a drug. It is in the form of a bullet, or preferably, a machete."

"Praise be to Allah, Sheik Creezin."

Chapter 37

It was 6:30 p.m. and I just arrived at our apartment. Mellie wasn't there, and I had no idea where she was. I knew she planned to do some heavy work on her latest book today and I didn't expect her to be away. She hadn't answered any of my calls, and my stomach was in a knot.

Five minutes later, Mellie walked in.

"Mel, honey, I've been calling your phone for hours, but you didn't answer. You look upset about something. What's up?"

"Sit, Max. I cannot fucking believe what I'm about to tell you. But first, why don't you make us a couple of martinis. I need some fortification."

Mellie usually prefers a glass of wine when she gets home. Her request for a martini told me something big was up. I mixed the drinks and we sat on the couch in the den.

"I was kidnapped, Max. You heard me, kidnapped. That's why I couldn't answer my phone. They took it from me. Yes, I was kidnapped. Kid—Fucking—Napped. But obviously it was only temporary."

I thought I'd pass out when Mellie said she was kidnapped. Mellie continued.

"As I was working on my book, the doorbell rang. I answered the door and opened it. I wasn't concerned because two guys in UPS uniforms stood there. Then, one of them pointed a gun at me and told me to accompany them downstairs to a waiting car. With a gun pointed at me, I wasn't in a position to argue. They took my phone and my gun. Once in the car one of the men put a hood over my head, obviously so I couldn't tell where they were taking me. Forty-five minutes later we got out of the car, me with a hood still over my head. One of the guys, I'll call him Jihadi Number One, took the hood off my head and seated me at a table in what appeared to be a kitchen in a suburban house. Then they hit me with the most bizarre plot I could ever imagine. They said that, from this day forward, I will need to submit every manuscript to them before sending it to my publisher. That's *every fucking manuscript*. Jihadi Number Two said that they would edit out any negative references to Islam if I hadn't already done so, which was also part of my 'assignment.' He also told me that I should write chapters that were favorable to radical Islam and terror. I was beginning to think it was some kind of a goddam joke— until they hit me with the convincer. If I refuse their demands, they will kill my sister, Nancy, or one of her three children who they named along with their ages: Jay, age 4, Mike, age 6, and Tommy, age 11. Yes, they knew their names and their ages. The bastards obviously did their research. One of the creeps, I think it was Jihadi Number One, laughed when he referred to their plan as *Editorial Terrorism*. They had also researched my writing habits and knew that I publish a book about every two months. He told me that if I simply stopped writing, they would continue with their plan to murder Nancy or the boys. He even gave me a list of deadlines—yes, deadlines—for submitting my manuscripts to them, along with a bunch of different email addresses which he said were untraceable. They told me that I would probably take their plan to the authorities, just as I'm now doing with you. 'No problem,' Jihadi Number Two said, chuckling, 'Tell whoever you want. Just be prepared to see your sister and her children killed if you don't follow our orders. We also have the family details for your two brothers. In other words, we've selected quite a few potential *targets* to enforce our demands.' Then they told me that they were about to return me to our apartment. When they let me off at the curb after removing my hood, they handed me my gun (without the bullets) and my cell phone. Then they both laughed—fucking laughed. So here I am."

After Mellie told me her story, I felt like someone just punched me in the stomach. *Editorial Terrorism?* The way Mellie just described the plan it could work. Actually, it was guaranteed to work because they would use family members as hostages. I asked Mellie for a license plate number, but the car was a rental. Then I asked if she would be able to identify the men from photographs. I was thinking about facial recognition software. But she said that the men were heavily made up. This was obviously a well-planned operation.

"Max, honey, do you think this plan can work?"

A logical question for an FBI agent. I figured I'd let Mellie answer her own question, as heart wrenching as it would be for her. I wanted to her to see the plan for the disgusting logic it carried.

"What do *you* think, Mellie?"

"I think that no author in her right mind can possibly resist their demands. I mean, who the hell would put her family in danger of being killed. I feel like I have a gun to my head, or more accurately, a gun to my sister's head, along with my three adorable nephews."

Unfortunately, Mellie was right. The *Editorial Terrorism* plan could work. It was brilliant, and cunning, and breathtakingly cruel. I reached for the phone.

"Who are you calling?"

"The *Silent Author Gang.* I'm calling a meeting for first thing in the morning."

I didn't want to tell Mellie that I was certain the terrorist plan could work. I think she already knew that—better than me.

Chapter 38

At 8:30 a.m. the *Silent Author Gang,* consisting of my sister Debbie, her husband Jason, and me convened in my office at 26 Federal Plaza. Mellie, of course, was there too. I asked FBI Director Watson and NYPD Commissioner Norquist to be there, but neither of them could make it. I planned to fill them in later.

I had just found out that Mellie's bodyguard was found behind our building. He was shackled and his mouth was taped. Thank God, he was alive. Obviously, the terrorists didn't want to complicate their plans with some violent criminality on the side.

Mellie and I filled them in on the terrorists' planned operation.

One look at Debbie's face told me she was upset about something. As a seasoned detective, my sister is good at wearing a poker face. But the look on her face told me she was bursting to tell us something, something important.

"You won't believe what I'm about to tell you," Debbie said after taking a deep breath. "The intake detective told me about a matter a few minutes ago, which is why I haven't told you yet.

Just yesterday a woman author, Janice McDonald, came forth with a horrifying story, a story like what Melanie just told us about, but worse, a lot worse. McDonald was approached by a couple of jihadis as you call them. They kidnapped her and took her to a secret location. But the kidnapping was only temporary, just as Melanie said. They told her pretty much what you said—submit your manuscript to us or we will attack your family. Janice McDonald, who is a complete asshole in my opinion, thought the jihadis were bluffing, so she submitted her latest manuscript to her publisher without jihadi approval, and without contacting the police or FBI. The book was, indeed, published. The day after the book was released, her husband was killed, brutally hacked to death with a machete in his office. This *Editorial Terrorism* is real, horribly real. If we can't figure out a way to stop this, don't expect to read anything even vaguely critical of Islam. The mouths of American authors have been silenced."

We all looked at Mellie, who sat there with a look on her face that can only be described as a combination of horror and anger.

"Pardon my silence," Mellie said, "but I'm just thinking about my sister Nancy and her three children. I'm the only person standing between them and violent death. And I've been given a deadline."

I reached over and grabbed her hand.

Then, Mellie described her "editorial" meeting with the jihadis as she had told me yesterday, including every detail. Mellie's typical personality is best described as outgoing and enthusiastic. Be she spoke in a monotone as she recounted her experience.

"Max, my brilliant brother, what are your thoughts?" Debbie said.

"We need to go after the editors, the jihadi editors," I said. "There's nothing to negotiate with those bastards. They just showed us how serious they are when they murdered Janice McDonald's husband. I'm taking the wraps off. This won't just be an investigation. This will be a battle, a violent battle."

Chapter 39

I called Buster and told him we needed to meet, and that Mellie would be with me. I suggested that Sarah Watson be there as well. Mellie and I took a 7:30 flight from JFK to Dulles Airport in Washington. I reserved seats in first class because I knew we had a lot to talk about and I wanted as much privacy as we could get on a commercial flight. We spoke softly, almost in a whisper.

Mellie was hurting, and when she hurts, I hurt. I wanted to make her pain go away, but I wasn't doing a good job of it. Somebody else was in control of the pain. I squeezed her hand and kissed her on the ear, which normally relaxes her. But the look on her face told me she was going through some bad stuff.

"There's a really simple solution to my problem," Mellie said, "simple as designed by those scumbags. All I need to do is write anything that doesn't criticize radical Islam. Just keep my mouth shut and do as I'm told."

"And how does that make you feel, honey?"

"I feel like I want to kill somebody. Just be a good little writer and obey orders. I'm not cut out that way, as you well know,

Max. But the lives of people in my family are at stake, and I feel like I'm in handcuffs. I think you're right as usual, baby, their plan will work. We saw just how it works with the murder of Janice McDonald's husband. We, I mean *you* law enforcement types, need to go after the jihadi editors. And you'll need a large body count. As you know, I'm not a fan of violence, Max, but you need to kill those bastards."

We arrived at CIA headquarters in Langley, Virginia at 10 a.m. Sarah Watson and Buster awaited us, along with my old friend from the FBI, Rick Bellamy, who Sarah had invited to the meeting. Rick is the Director of the FBI Counterterrorism Task Force. Yes, counterterrorism is the subject of this meeting. I've worked with Rick many times on various cases that involved terrorism. He's a good guy, competent as hell, and I like him. He doesn't try to micromanage me when I'm working a case, and I appreciate that. He trusts me as I trust him.

Buster called the meeting to order.

"From what Max has told me, we're looking at a cluster fuck of gargantuan proportions," Buster said with his customary bluntness. "I'm going to ask my favorite author to bring us up to date. Mellie?"

"In the past two days," Mellie said, "I've told this story to Max as well as our *Silent Author Gang*, which consists of Max, his sister, and his brother-in-law. I'll try not to puke as I tell it once again."

Mellie recounted for us her experience so far with *Editorial Terrorism*, it's demands and its threats against the lives of her sister and three nephews. The murder of the husband of a famous author, Janice McDonald, put an exclamation point behind

Mellie's story. Janice didn't do as she was told, and a vicious murder resulted.

"One thing about this plan," Mellie continued, "is that it's quite simple, unlike some of the cases you guys handle. The simple fact is that I have no choice, absolutely no choice— unless I want my sister and possibly her children killed. Janice McDonald thought she had a choice, and she made the wrong one. It got her husband brutally murdered, hacked to death with a machete. So, I have a deadline two months from now, and I know exactly what I need to do. First, I need to go back over what I've already written and take out any parts of the book that in any way criticize Islam, and then make sure that I don't write any more such stuff. So that's my choice and I'm taking it. I have to take it. No way in hell will I risk the lives of Nancy, Jay, Mike, or Tommy. Yes, their plan is already underway in my brain, of which I'm no longer in control. So that's the simple part of the case, curb my writing. It gets complicated when you consider that these animals have just taped the mouths of me and all other authors across the country. Our words no longer belong to us but to the killers in charge. I promised not to puke, but I'm rethinking that. Folks, we've just entered a new era in American literature, the era of fucking *Editorial Terrorism*. Your thoughts, Buster?"

Buster looked angry. He's usually good at keeping his emotions covered up, the it was obvious that he was pissed.

"Just as the jihadi plan is simple, so is mine," Buster said. "My people are going to have a chat with a few folks."

From my past dealings with Buster, I knew exactly what he meant. A "chat,' as he uses the word, means that some people are going to get killed.

"Buster," Sarah Watson said, "are you going to meet with 'our friend?'"

Our friend, as we all know, is Buster's star insider, his secret mole. The person's identity is so secret that few people know who he is, including me. Buster knows how to protect his insiders. I soon found out that I will be one of the few people who knows who "our friend" is. I guess I should feel flattered by being brought so far inside, but I was nervous as hell.

We'd soon meet with "our friend."

Chapter 40

At 11:45 a.m. on a bright sunny morning, I went to the Bethesda Terrace, a beautifully situated restaurant on Bethesda Lake in Central Park. I recalled my parents taking me there once when I was a teenager, and I love the place. Buster told me that this restaurant was the normal spot to meet with "our friend." We sat at a table on the outside deck, which provided a nice view as well as a space for private conversations. I was to meet with Buster, Rick Bellamy, the Counterterrorism honcho from the FBI, and "our friend." His identity is so secret I couldn't even tell Mellie about it. Mellie gets it. Although we share everything with each other, she understands the spy doctrine of "need to know." It's a way of keeping secrets just that, secret. If someone without a need to know possesses secret information, there's the chance that he or she might blurt it out without thinking. "Loose lips sink ships" and all that. Sometimes, during a conversation, Mellie would hold a finger to her lips and say, "I don't think I need to know that." She's the best.

As Buster, Rick, and I sipped our coffee, a tall heavy-set priest walked up to our table. My God, this guy was huge. He looked like a professional wrestler under his priestly attire. We're going to be meeting with a priest? Buster had told me that "our friend" is well known, among the few people who know him, as a master of disguises. This guy knows how to stay undercover.

"Max, meet Imam Mike. Mike, this is our friend, FBI Agent Max Wakefield." The guy offered me a huge, beefy hand.

Imam Mike, aka Muhammed Busharif, is the religious leader, or Imam, of a mosque in Brooklyn. He's a trusted inside source, one of the best the FBI or the CIA has, if not *the* best. He gradually became infuriated with all of the terrorist killings in the name of his religion. When a good friend of his daughter was killed in a bomb attack at a football game, Mike went over the edge. He renounced his religion, but only to a select few people, including Buster, Rick Bellamy, and now me. Mike's language tends to be salty, not what you'd expect from a religious leader. Mike's on our side and is probably the most important mole we've ever had, according to Buster. Buster told me that Mike feeds us information that we could never get without an insider like him. Although he's not a professional, he operates like a seasoned spy. When he delivers a sermon in his mosque, he's careful to avoid any subject that's even mildly political. The last thing he could afford to do was be labeled as "a reformer." He had an imam friend in Westchester, a "reformer" like himself, who would openly denounce the radicals in his sermons. The man is no longer among the living. Mike knows better. In his sermons he sticks to discussions of family matters, friendships, and religious observances. Mike knows how to remain invisible. He's also a good guy and easy to get along with.

"Mike," Buster said, "can you tell us anything about a jihadi project known as *Editorial Terrorism*?" Mike's eyes flitted around the deck. He knows how to be careful and how to keep the lid on sensitive information.

"That's what I called you about yesterday, Buster, although

I didn't mention the name of the project, of course. This is one of the wildest fucking jihadi operations I've ever seen. They're trying to muzzle American authors to prevent them from writing anything critical of the radical elements of that lovely religion. On Buster's suggestion, I read one of your wife's books, Max, and I loved it. Besides being a very pretty woman, she is one tremendous writer. I shared it with my wife and now she's a Melanie Pierce fan too. I noticed that your wife often mentions Ayaan Hirsi Ali, a reformer like me. Your wife is quite a brave woman, but her bravery will not stop the *Editorial Terrorism* shit. Buster tells me that she's one of the targets of our friendly terrorists."

"Yes, my wife a target," I said. "The jihadi folks have threatened to kill her sister and three nephews unless she submits her books for 'editorial review.' Melanie, or Mellie as I call her, is beside herself. She's a tough, courageous woman, but when her family is threatened, she thinks she has no choice but to comply with the radicals' demands. She has been given a deadline for submitting her 'cleaned-up' manuscript. In other words, the lives of her sister and nephews are in her hands and she has two months to do as ordered. Is there anything you can tell us, Mike?"

"Fortunately, the radical assholes who inhabit my mosque don't know how to keep their mouths shut. Yes, in answer to your question, Max," Mike said, "I have five names and I was also able to find their addresses, if you can believe that. From what I hear there are a total of 26 jihadis involved in the project, a pretty large number for one of their operations. Although their collective IQs are the equivalent of a fucking fruit bat, they're smart enough not to meet regularly in a specific place. The operation is run by an outfit known as The Committee. They communicate primarily by email—as if I don't know how to hack emails. If they met in person regularly, Buster over here could conduct one of his famous raids, but it won't be that easy. But hey, I've only been tracking this project for about a week, ever since I first heard the words *Editorial Terrorism*. But don't worry, I know how to keep my ears open and my mouth shut. I expect that we'll learn a lot more about this sicko project as the days go by. Here are the names and addresses I've gotten. I assume they're the leaders of the project from the way they communicate."

He handed a piece of paper to Buster.

"I recognize a few of these names from the CIA watch list," Buster said.

"Mike, do you know how they get the names of the targets, the family members of the authors?" Rick Bellamy asked.

"Yeah, it's a real bitch. Ever hear of Facebook? We Americans enjoy sharing personal information over the Internet. I'm afraid that we love to fuck ourselves."

"Your recommendation, Mike?" Buster said.

"We need more information. Let me put my listening ears on and let's meet back here in exactly one week."

"What will be your disguise, Mike?" Rick Bellamy said.

"That will be our little secret—until I meet you here."

Chapter 41

Mellie is under more stress than I've ever seen. She's one of the greatest writers in the country, if not the world, but now she writes with a gag order over her fingers. Her thoughts and ideas have captured the hearts of readers around the globe, but now her thoughts and ideas are no longer hers alone; they must be reviewed by an Editorial Terrorist. It's tearing Mellie apart, but there's nothing we can do about it at the present.

I decided she needed to relax, so I suggested we go to our house in Amagansett, always a great place to relieve stress. Tomorrow is Friday so we'll head out then. Mellie's amazing talent has made us rich, so rich that we could kick back and do nothing if we were so inclined. But we're not so inclined. I love my career in the FBI and Mellie loves to write, even with a muzzle. So, we spend money by hiring limos rather than renting cars.

We got to Amagansett at 11:30 a.m. on Friday morning. It was a perfect mid-June day, with a temperature in the low 80s. I called a local gourmet deli and had lunch delivered so we could sit on the deck overlooking the ocean.

Mellie wanted to talk, and I wanted her to. Keeping negative feelings bottled up results in bottled-up feelings, a bad way to live a life.

"I recently reviewed all of my 25 books, Max, and I discovered something interesting. Only 10 of my books contain anything critical of radical Islam. That's only 40 percent of my writing. But the thing that kills me is that each of those books hit number one on the best seller list. They are the best sellers of my best sellers. If it were completely up to my publisher, all my books would be Islam-negative. Could I do all my writing without a word of criticism of radical Islamism? Of course. Many good writers never touch the subject because it's not something that interests them. But you've seen me work, honey. When a story shows up in my brain—and that's how it happens—a story *shows up*, my heart needs to follow it. I can't do that anymore. I have to self-edit myself or the bastards will kill one of my family. Does that impact my writing? It sure does. I've noticed in the past week that my writing has suffered, even if I'm not writing about anything to do with Islam. I feel like I have a fucking muzzle on my fingers. I find myself slaving over every word, not for grammar or style, but for its content, content over which I have no control."

"Mellie, I've watched you work and it's inspiring, and you know I'm not bullshitting you. Although I can't read your mind—I'm working on that—I can see in your face when you just came up with something great. I flatter you because you are great, one of the greatest writers in the friggin world. So, what do you think, Mellie? I know when I flatter you like crazy it makes you horny, but it's not just when I want to get laid. I flatter you because I mean it."

"Wanna get laid?"

"Of course, I do, but don't be a wiseass. Hey, let's look at this positively. This *Editorial Terrorism* shit is at the top of the agendas at both the CIA and FBI. No way in hell will the United States government put up with allowing authors to be censored. Although I can't tell you his name, I met with that guy who's known as 'our friend.' (*Imam Mike*). The guy is amazing. He's already come up with not only ideas but leads. You heard me—leads. Just like our friend Trevor got your $20 million back, when great minds are on the case, shit happens, good shit."

I felt relieved. The look on Mellie's face told me I'd gotten to her with the most important thing I could say—I gave her *hope*. I could see the stress disappear from her face. She looked at me and gave me one of her beautiful smiles, a devilish smile, which always drives me crazy. You'd think I would get used to that, but it never happened. One smile from Mellie and I go into testosterone- melt-down mode.

"So, getting back to my question a few minutes ago, honey," Mellie said, "Wanna get laid?"

"I thought you'd never ask."

Chapter 42

I just got a call from none other than Ellen Bellamy, the famous TV personality, the host of *The Ellen Bellamy Show,* the most popular talk show on daytime television. I've met Ellen on a few occasions, and I really like her. I think of her as a friend, and I believe she sees me that way too. She's the wife of Rick Bellamy, a friend and colleague of Max at the FBI. Rick is the Director of the Counterterrorism Task Force, and it was his idea for Ellen to call me. Max and I have had dinner with the Bellamys a few times. Normally, a booking producer would reach out, but Ellen decided to make the call herself because we know each other. She's a pro.

Ellen is a lovely blond, and she has a personality that draws viewers like honey draws bees. When she asks questions, the viewing audience listens, and the interviewee talks. She was once a successful architect, but a CBS producer saw one of her speeches at a convention, and realized he discovered a new TV talent. He got it right.

Ellen wanted to interview me about, what else, *Editorial Terrorism*.

I've been interviewed on TV countless times, including Ellen's show, and I love to appear because it sells a ton of my books. My agent sets up most of them. But this request was different. My speaking out about *Editorial Terrorism* could get people killed, especially some of my family members. Ellen gets it, and her FBI agent husband, Rick, had alerted her to be cautious. I wouldn't be interviewed by my name, and I'd be heavily made up and recorded with trick videography. I would speak through a voiceover—a male voice. I would be introduced, not as Melanie Pierce, but as a "famous best-selling author." My gender would not be identified.

After Ellen explained the security measures, I jumped at the idea. Obviously, my appearance on her show wouldn't sell any books because my name wouldn't be mentioned, but it would help get the word out to the American public just what this *Editorial Terrorism* shit was all about. And did I ever want to get that story out.

Max insisted, and Rick backed him up on it, that we could review the tape before it aired.

When we looked at the tape, we were fine with it, although it was hard to watch because Max was laughing so hard. I looked like Elmo the Clown and I sounded like Darth Vader.

"Good evening ladies and gentlemen and welcome to *The Ellen Bellamy Show*. I'm your host, you guessed it, Ellen Bellamy. My guest this afternoon is a famous best-selling author who has a startling if not terrifying story to tell. The subject this author will discuss has become known as *Editorial Terrorism*, a nefarious plot to silence the nation's authors and prevent them from writing anything critical of radical Islam in their books. That's why my guest is heavily made up and his or her voice is disguised."

The camera panned to a joint shot of Ellen and me, although

you would never know it was me.

"Welcome to *The Ellen Bellamy Show*, Melanie (bleeped out.) Please tell us about this project called *Editorial Terrorism*.

"Quite simply" I said, sounding like Darth Vader lecturing Luke Skywalker, "*Editorial Terrorism* is just that, terrorism. Authors are told that they must submit a draft of their books so the terrorists can review them to make sure there are no negative references to radical Islam. If an author refuses the demand, one of his or her family members will be killed. The tragic case of Janice McDonald is the most dramatic example of their operation." I felt myself getting nauseous when I mentioned the Janice McDonald matter. "Thinking that the terrorists were bluffing, Ms. McDonald refused to submit her book. When it was published, her husband was brutally murdered, hacked to death with a machete in his office. Besides self-editing under the watchful eye of the terrorists, authors are expected to write words in praise of radical extremism. The project is brilliant if unspeakably cruel. No authors in their right mind would fail to submit to the terrorists demands and see a family member slain. And to simply stop writing isn't an option. The terrorists keep a list of publishing schedules for all the authors and give the author a deadline. If the manuscript isn't submitted by the deadline date, a family member is killed."

"What do you think can be done about this horrible project?" Ellen said (she almost said my name again).

"There's little to nothing that authors can do, other than obey the commands of the terrorists. We're hostages, or rather our family members are hostages,"

I hoped I was getting through to the viewers.

"Thank you for joining us on our show this afternoon, and I wish you the best for your suddenly dangerous career as a novelist.

Most of you folks know that my husband Rick, is Director of the FBI Counterterrorism Task Force. He tells me, for publication, that this *Editorial Terrorism* matter is at the top of the FBI's list of urgent cases. Rick will join me tomorrow afternoon to discuss the issue further. Hope you will all join us again tomorrow afternoon for another edition of *The Ellen Bellamy Show*. This is Ellen Bellamy saying so long for now."

"So how did you think the show went, Max? I know we looked at the tape in advance, but I'd like to hear your latest reaction."

"I thought you were fabulous, honey, even though you looked like a clown and sounded like a movie monster. I think you got the story across perfectly, that American authors are being silenced by terrorists. I always thought it was a great idea for you to be booked on TV talk shows because it sells books by the truckload. But with this *Editorial Terrorism* shit, you performed one the most important public services possible. You're not only a great writer, but a great American. I'm proud of you, honey, as usual."

"Do you think I should try to get booked on more shows like this one?"

"Yes, I was going to suggest that. As long as your name is anonymous and you're heavily disguised I don't see any danger. I think you should round up some of your fellow best-selling pals and hit the airwaves. I think it's critically important that you guys let the reading public know that you're not in control of what you write, that it's not you who is doing the censoring."

"And what are you FBI guys going to do?"

"You know I can't be specific with you, honey, but let me just say that you can expect to see a lot of jihadis go underground—six feet underground."

Chapter 43

Because my negative opinions of radical Islam have been effectively muzzled, I turned my attention to writing about the remnants of the Mafia, a group of creeps who often act like terrorists. For the time being, any criticism of Islamic terrorism would come from journalists, not from fiction writers. This sucks, but I'm stuck with it.

Max introduced me to a couple of interesting (and famous) NYPD cops with whom he'd worked on joint cases with the FBI, Bobbie Nelson and her husband Bob Lawton. A few of the cases they worked on involved intimate contact with the Mafia. They're probably the two most well-known detectives in the country, and *The New York Times* labeled them the "BBs." I thought that was cool, because Max and I are known as the M&Ms, although we've not been so christened by *The New York Times*. The *Times* also referred to them as *"New York's Dynamic Detective Duo."* Holy shit, indeed they are hot stuff. But I would soon find that they're really nice people, easy to like and enjoy their company.

They're good friends with Max's NYPD detective sister Debbie, who filled us in about them. Bobbie Nelson had been hired away from the Chicago Police Department during the famous NYPD fiasco in which hundreds of NYPD cops were arrested in a bribery scandal. *The Chicago Tribune* called Bobbie "a real life Sherlock Holmes."

Their background story was sweet. Both Detectives First Grade with the NYPD, they were partnered by police Commissioner Ralph Norquist. After working together a short while, they fell in love and married. Like me, Bobbie decided to keep her maiden name in marriage. Bobbie Nelson was quite famous, and many magazine articles having been written about her. Her name helped her and Bob to land a publishing contract for what would become a best-selling nonfiction book entitled *Detectiving*, which, as the name implies, is all about the profession of being a detective. The book made, and is making, a fortune. It's pretty much required reading for any detective or would-be detective in the U.S. They had a brief red-hot romance, followed by a vow of life together. Their story was reminiscent of Max and me, although we're not cops. An author friend of mine even wrote a book about them titled *Puzzles*, because that's what they're so good at solving. Shit, I wish I had a crack at writing that book, even though it was nonfiction, not a novel. But it read like a novel, and I loved it, giving it a rave review. No doubt about it, they are one interesting couple. Max and I discovered that we just found a couple of new friends when we had lunch with them.

We invited Bob and Bobbie to visit our place in Amagansett, only about three miles from their vacation home in East Hampton. Like us, they also have an apartment in Manhattan. Their book royalties provide for a few luxuries, as I well know. Bob Lawton was also a best-selling author of a police novel, *An Army of Blue*. At our invitation, they brought along their two-year-old adopted daughter, Tilly, their one-year-old son, James, their delightful and pretty governess Jane, and their crazy French Bulldog, Lucky. I can't remember the last time we invited such fun guests.

They told us that amorous little Lucky had knocked up an East Hampton neighbor's dog, which recently gave birth to a litter of four puppies. At least the other dog was also a French Bulldog, so the puppies would be purebred. Their neighbor enlisted Bobbie and Bob's help in finding a home for the puppies. Bobbie, who loves dogs, thought she saw in me a kindred spirit as little Lucky sat on my lap, slurping my face.

"Melanie, you must be lonely in your big apartment as you write your novels. You could use some canine company."

It was an idea I had toyed with from time to time but never acted on it. Hell, I work out of our apartment, which is huge. I can walk the dog in our big rooftop garden. And I sure can use some friendly company during the day. Why not? We agreed to visit their neighbor later that afternoon so I could check out the puppies. Max, a dog lover himself, thought the idea was excellent.

We spent the next few hours discussing the Mafia. My God, those two are super detectives. They recalled every detail of their experiences with the mob, each one of which would make a great book. Being a fanatical note taker, I wrote down enough information to fill a book with my notes alone. I had discussed the idea of my writing about the mob with my agent, Jack Melton. He loved the idea. Exciting stories sell books. After my learning session with the BBs, I felt like I was a junior mafioso. No surprise, some story ideas already started percolating in my brain.

After our meeting, we went to East Hampton to visit the neighbor with the puppies for adoption. Lily Franken answered the door. I think she spied me as a puppy magnet as soon as she looked at me. She took us to a back room where her dog, Foxy, was napping with the puppies. I looked at the little squirmies and immediately fell in love with an adorable female with a tan coat. Her chest was white as well as her paws. Her broad little face seemed to carry a permanent smile. I immediately thought of a name, "Mine."

Lily, a diligent accountant, had all the paperwork we needed including the time for the puppy's next shots. I scooped up the little bundle and cradled her in my arms. The puppy seemed to love me as much as I loved her.

On our way back to our house, Max and I agreed that her name would be *Maggie*, reminiscent of Amagansett, a bit more appropriate than the name "Mine." Little Maggie snuggled in my lap as my heart fluttered. Max reached over and tickled her behind the ear. We looked at each other and both said, "Good move."

Bobbie invited us to their house Sunday for a barbecue and we immediately said yes. I think these two are becoming friends, especially since they brokered us into a relationship with adorable little Maggie.

We had a great time with Bob and Bobbie's fun family. Their governess, Jane, is also a serious novelist, and loves to work for them because she has time to write when the two little ones are sleeping. Jane had recently had a book published by none other than Penguin Random House, my usual publisher. So, we had lunch with three authors besides myself. Our conversation, naturally, got around to *Editorial Terrorism* and the *Silent Author Case,* which Max was handling as the lead FBI agent. Little Maggie sat on my lap under the watchful eye of her father, Lucky.

The *Silent Author* Case is anything but secret, so we discussed it openly. Bob and Bobbie, two superstar detectives, said that they would ask Commissioner Norquist if they could work the case. I thought Max would do a cartwheel, and I felt like joining him. The idea of the famous BBs working the *Silent Author Case* made the day for us. Max knows Commissioner Norquist well and told the BBs that he'd be happy to back them up in their application. Norquist knows his superstars well, and usually follows their assignment requests.

Bob and Bobbie both said they'd love to work with Max, having gotten to know him after our weekend with them. And they're good friends with Max's sister, Detective Debbie.

So, the BBs may work the *Silent Author Case*. Wow.

Chapter 44

When we got back to New York after our great weekend in Amagansett, I couldn't wait to start scribbling ideas for my new book, my first Mafia novel. The title will be *An Assignment in Hell*. Often, I don't come up with a title until I'm half-way or more into a book, but Bobbie and Bob's detailed descriptions of their cases made for an almost fully-formed novel in my head, an unusual occurrence. But my first job was to acquaint little Maggie with her new city home. I took her to our rooftop garden which included a lawn area. Maggie is a small breed, often referred to not as a toy, but by the wonderful name "teacup." Max and I played with calling her teacup, but my research (of course) told me that teacup was an overly used name for small dogs. So, in our desire to be different, we named her Maggie, which played well alliteratively with Amagansett. When I set her down in the garden she looked at me and seemed to get it. She immediately piddled and then did number two. It was such a tiny load I could clean up after her by using a teaspoon to flick her stuff into the bushes.

I sat down at my computer and started to jot down ideas with Maggie sitting on my lap. Max prepared dinner. He loves to cook as much as I do, and he's really good at it. He's amazing how he knows from memory just the right spices to use. Have I mentioned that I married well?

An Assignment from Hell began to formulate in my brain. It was patterned after a case the BBs actually worked on, an exciting and scary assignment. The names of the heroes, of course, were different—Jack and Jane not the real Bob and Bobbie. They were assigned to a stakeout job in Chicago, on loan to the FBI. The purpose of the stakeout was to gather information on Mafia activities and plans. Every day, they would sit and have lunch at a place that was known as a Mafia hangout and record nearby mob conversations using a highly sensitive recording device. They did a great job, providing the FBI with previously unknown details on Mafia plans and actions. Their work, however, was too good. The Mafia caught on to them, noticing that they always had lunch at a mob-hangout restaurant. Mob management even circulated photos of them with and without their disguises. The FBI Director discovered that their covers had been blown and ordered them to return to New York immediately. But Jane was forcibly kidnapped as she visited the ladies' room at O'Hare airport. It was a horrifying time for Jane (Bobbie), and the experience was embellished, of course, by additional side stories from my novelist's brain. Jane, the damsel in distress, is saved, of course, by her brave husband/partner Jack (Bob). Great story line, and I was having a blast telling it. Little Maggie seemed to detect my enthusiasm and occasionally put her paws on my chest so I could lift her up to slurp my face.

Max, always my first editor, reviewed the story so far, although it wasn't close to being finished. Dinner was heating on the stove as Max sat down and read.

"This is great stuff, Mellie, which is no surprise. You seem to have internalized everything Bob and Bobbie told you about the Mafia. But I have a question. Do you feel like you're being cut off from something, namely your stories about radical Islam?"

Max, as usual, nailed it. Yes, I was having a good time writing about the mob, especially after my fascinating interview with Bob and Bobbie, but something was missing. What was missing was my sense of freedom to write what is really on my mind. I can't escape the feeling that my writing is being controlled by someone else, someone who will kill my family if I don't follow orders. The feeling sucked, but there's nothing I can do about it.

The next day we got great news. NYPD Commissioner Norquist assigned Bobbie Nelson and Bob Lawton to work on the *Silent Author Case*. Both Max and I were happy as hell that two best-selling authors as well as great detectives would have a chance to turn their writers' anger toward the editorial scumbags who want to silence American authors.

The question constantly on my mind is how long my fellow writers and I will be stuck with *Editorial Terrorism*.

Chapter 45

I finished writing *An Assignment in Hell* in record time of five weeks. With the factual details provided to me by Bobbie Nelson and Bob Lawton, the words seemed to fly out of my fingers. I submitted the manuscript to my girls, who all returned it in their normal time of one week. Then I gave it to Max, my favorite editor. Of course, I also submitted it to the *Editorial Terrorism* scumbags who control my thoughts.

Max finished his review in two nights. He loved it, and he never throws praise unless he means it. He flattered the hell out of me, which I promised I'd thank him for later in the bedroom. Am I nuts to get horny whenever my irresistible husband flatters me? Maybe, but sex with Max is a nice kind of nuts.

Finally, I submitted it to my literary agent, Jack Melton. He had already cleared the story concept with my publisher, Penguin Random House. He got me a million-dollar advance, even though the subject matter isn't my usual stuff. Jack Melton is definitely a keeper as an agent.

In one month, the book was ready to be published. Penguin works fast on doing the final editorial comments for my books.

They work fast because, after my girls, Max, Mom, and Sheila, not to mention my careful rewriting, they get a manuscript from me that's already highly polished and just about ready to launch.

I was happy as hell that, within two weeks of publication, the book hit the best-seller list at number eight. The following week it was number two, then number one the week after that.

So, it looks like I can hit one out of the park without touching on radical Islam. But I still hate to be under the control of somebody other than my publisher. At least I'm making money—lots of it.

Chapter 46

Mustaffa Creezin met with his undercover jihadi comrade, Ali Chudori (Harry Paxton) in Chudori's apartment in Manhattan. The subject of their meeting was the exciting, and highly successful project, *Editorial Terrorism*.

"Our project is working as planned, Ali. The authors are obeying our dictates and don't mention a word critical of Islam. Even that best-selling bitch Melanie Pierce is now following our orders. Her latest book is about the Mafia, and it's ranked number one on *The New York Times* best seller list. Maybe she will realize that she can keep her successful career without writing any negative thoughts on Islam. To keep her encouraged, we have added 15 potential targets to hit if she doesn't follow our demands."

"Are those additional family members?"

"No, they are a group of elderly women to whom Melanie Pierce refers as 'my girls.' She's quite fond of them and uses them as beta readers, informal editors. Not to worry my brother, Melanie Pierce will behave herself."

"Our editors have reviewed 73 books in the last two months

alone, and those books were written by critics of Islam, staunch critics. Each and every one of the books has passed our editorial demands. It appears that our plan is working perfectly. It's accurate to say that no new books are being published that are in any way critical of our holy religion. The project is perfect."

"I question, Sheik Mustaffa, if it's accurate to say that any project is perfect. Something always seems to go wrong. But I will say this. I have never seen a project work so well, one that successfully carries out our objectives."

"We must keep in mind, Ali, that the only reason why Melanie Pierce and her fellow big-selling authors are following our demands is because they have no choice. Our swift action with that woman Janice McDonald put an exclamation point on our plans. She thought we were bluffing, and her husband paid the price with his life. My insiders tell me that she's writing a children's novel about an adventure of squirrels living in a forest, and her publisher has approved her agent's plans for six more children's books. She learned her lesson—the hard way. But the important thing is that she did learn her lesson."

Mustaffa laughed when Ali told him about the children's book being written by a former harsh critic of Islam.

"We must face one large problem, Ali, the Australian bank examiner named Trevor McMartin. The man is a genius at tracking down exchanges of money. As you know, he discovered the location of Melanie Pierce's funds and arranged for all the money to be returned to her. She got her $20 million back."

"Our brothers on The Committee have come up with a solution to the Trevor McMartin problem. From now on, all funds that we manage to embezzle are immediately converted into gold. No way can he trace that. That bank examiner should find himself a new way of making a living."

"Yes, Ali, our *Editorial Terrorism* team has found a pot of gold."

"And let us continue to fill the pots."

Chapter 47

G'day, Mate. Yer ole friend Trevah's got some interesting news for ya."

"Trevor, good to hear from you," Rick Bellamy said. "How's my favorite bank examiner doing? What's up?"

"Our ole friends, the terrorists on The Committee, are up to some new plans, some really stupid new plans. Can I stop by your office now? I don't feel comfortable talking to you on the phone about this new situation."

Rick Bellamy loved to get together with his old friend, the eccentric and brilliant Australian bank Examiner, Trevor McMartin. Trevor has a way of solving cases that are beyond the typical detective.

"Rick, you once told me that that fellow, whose name I don't know, the guy you refer to as 'our friend," once said that the radicals in charge of The Committee have the 'collective intelligence of a fruit bat.' Well, your friend is correct. They are collectively stupid, devious but stupid. They're so stupid they think they can pull the wool over ole Trevah's eyes. Never will happen, Mate. The Committee blokes think they can hide their fund transfers by investing in gold. So, I tracked down each and every one of their transfers, and I've even located the gold certificates. We haven't acted on any of my evidence so far because we want to make a gigantic transfer all at once. And here's news that will make your ears happy. From my tracking of correspondence, I believe they may be planning on holding a meeting of everyone involved in the *Editorial Terrorism*. You heard me, Mate, a bleeping meeting. That's all the information I have right now. Maybe your 'friend' can give you more information. I understand that, whoever he is, has got his ear to the ground. I'm sure you and your mates would love to attend a meeting of The Committee. I do 90 percent of my work online. But you blokes do your works with guns drawn. I suggest you take off the safeties, Mate."

"Trevor, as always, think you for your excellent work. Yes, I will talk to 'our friend' about any possible meeting plans."

Chapter 48

Max, it's Rick. We'll be meeting with 'our friend,' tomorrow at noon at our usual place, four days before our next scheduled meeting on the specific request of our friend himself. Buster plans to be there as well. 'Our friend' sounds like he has something big to discuss."

I was excited that Rick called me about our next meeting with Imam Mike, one that Mike himself requested. Mike wouldn't request a meeting not on the regular schedule unless he had something big to tell us. I was excited but nervous. Mike knows how to get things done, and that's what I'm hoping for, to get things done. I've been worried about Mellie. Although her books are selling like hot dogs at a ballgame, she's not her usual self. Although she's making a ton of money, the dollars are never what motivates her. She's a pro, one of the best writers in the world, and although the hot book sales tell her she's doing a good job, it still grates at her to have a lock on her keyboard, a lock for which editorial terrorists have the key. Having discovered a while ago that Mellie is the most important part of my life, I've dedicated myself to do whatever is in my (limited) power to help free her and her fellow authors. As Buster said, I not only owe it to her, I owe it to the writers and readers of the world.

———— ● ————

At 11:45 on a bright Wednesday morning, Rick Bellamy, Buster, and I sat at an end table on the outside deck of the Bethesda Terrace restaurant overlooking the lake in Central Park. We waited for Imam Mike to appear, wondering what his latest disguise would be.

A tall, heavy woman with huge shoulders walked over to our table. She was wearing a large flowing green dress and huge flat shoes that looked as big as the boats on the lake.

"Hi guys," she said with a deep falsetto voice. "Yes, I'd love a beer."

Although I was new to this relationship, I began to enjoy Imam Mike and his disguises, but more importantly, his inside information. He didn't disappoint us.

After taking a swig of his beer, Mike hit us with some wonderfully shocking information.

"The assholes on The Committee are even dumber than I originally thought. They're planning a meeting with all 26 of the *Editorial Terrorism* folks. You heard me, a meeting, a fucking meeting."

"Where will it be, Mike?" Buster asked, his eyes bugging out of his head.

"Saugerties, New York," Mike said, "a sleepy little town in Ulster County. Part of the town is inside Catskill Park. The meeting will be held in the Village of Saugerties two weeks from now at private house they rented. Here's the address."

He handed me a piece of paper.

"I'll have my assistant rent a house nearby, hopefully next door," I said.

Looks like it's time to take the safeties off our guns.

"From the conversations I heard," Mike said, "they chose Saugerties because it's out of the way and doesn't see large crowds. So, I guess you guys are going to *swat* some flies."

By swat, Mike was referring to a SWAT team, the acronym for Special Weapons and Tactics. All major police departments as well as the 56 FBI field offices around the country have SWAT teams at their disposal. SWAT teams are used for high risk situations, such as hostage incidents. A SWAT team mission is more of a military type action than a typical law enforcement operation. Given the seriousness of the *Editorial Terrorism*, I think Rick Bellamy is right on target to use a SWAT, an *Enhanced* SWAT team no less. An *Enhanced* SWAT is a force of 40 officers and heavy-duty weapons, including MP5/10mm machine guns, M4 carbines, and rocket launchers. Imam Mike refers to a SWAT team as "a mean bunch of motherfuckers," and he's right. Rick told us he intends to use an enhanced team because of the large number of people involved. Twenty-six is a lot of terrorists to handle. Rick doesn't want to blow this one and neither do I. I will be at the "safe house" in Saugerties when we arrange to rent one, but I won't be involved in the actual attack, assuming there will be an attack. With luck I won't get my head blown off as I came close to in the past.

Two weeks from now the meeting will be held, the meeting where we'll edit the editors.

Chapter 49

In two days, I will hold my annual meeting with "my girls." I love to get together with them socially because they're such a fun group. We will meet at Cipriani's on 42nd Street, one of my all-time favorite restaurants. It touts itself as "simple, elegant, good food," and I agree. The promotions don't mention that it's expensive as hell, but that's okay, my girls deserve the best, and I can certainly afford it. The Cipriani group of restaurants began with a bar in Venice, Italy in 1931 named Harry's Bar, and it still exists today. It was named after Harry Pickering, the American founder. The place was run by Giuseppe Cipriani, hence the Cipriani name for the group of restaurants. My girls love to hear the history of Harry's Bar, which was a haunt of the rich and famous from the arts, including Ernest Hemingway, Charlie Chaplin, Alfred Hitchcock, Truman Capote, and Orson Welles, among countless others. I love to give my girls a treat in addition to the huge amount of money I pay them.

From what I can glean, something big is going to happen with the FBI in a couple of weeks. Max, of course, did not give me any details at all because of the famous "need to know doctrine," which makes a lot of sense, even though my inquiring mind doesn't like secretiveness. The fewer the people who know of a secret, the better are the chances that it will remain a secret. But my detective/writer brain told me that something big is coming up. I'll just keep my mouth shut and hope for the best. With Max on the case, it's easy to hope for the best. FBI Director Sarah Watson once told me that Max is the best agent in the Bureau. I don't think she was saying that to be nice because she said it in front of a few other people. She may think he's the best in the Bureau, but I just think he's the best, period.

The identity of my girls is hardly a secret, which worries me a bit, and worries Max a lot. One of my terrorist editors told me that my girls have been added to the list of potential targets if I don't follow instructions. Those bastards know how to get me to follow orders.

Eighty-year-old Babs Holden has christened herself the head cheerleader for the girls. She even runs a Facebook page about the girls, a site well-known in writing circles. Babs is a technical whiz, having once worked as a programmer for Google. Unlike most of my girls, Babs is financially secure with a decent pension. She donates every penny I pay her for reviewing my manuscripts to the NYU writing department. Under her technical eye, Babs coached all of my girls to use texting and email for our communications. She even taught them to use Zoom and Go-To-Meeting.com so we can have occasional face to face online editorial meetings. A lot of my fellow authors have formed beta groups like my girls to pre-read their manuscripts, although none of them pay the kind of money I do.

All my girls take a proprietary interest in the success of my books, and they even help a lot with promotion, always a good thing. Babs even creates a separate webpage for each of each of my books in addition to the ones my publisher puts out. All of Babs' pages for my novels begin with the words, "Read Now," such as "Read Now-*The Shadows of Terror*."

I was concerned that the meeting would get around to a discussion of the writing world's worst-kept secret, *Editorial Terrorism*. My concern was well-founded, because my girls didn't seem to want to talk about anything else. They simply hated the idea that any of my books would be censored, because they love my books, no matter what the subject. Hell, if I wrote a book about a cat weaning her kittens, my girls would love it. One of them even inquired if it was me on *The Ellen Bellamy Show*, where I was dressed like Elmo the Clown and spoke like Darth Vader. Top secret, of course, and I denied it. Max has taught me the importance of keeping your cover on tight.

I tried to steer the conversation to my latest novel, *The Shadows of Terror*. The book is kicking ass on all the best-seller lists, and I thought that subject may be more interesting than *Editorial Terrorism*. I was only somewhat successful, because my girls really wanted to talk about literary censorship. They all hate the very idea of some group putting a muzzle on authors, almost as much as I hate it. Well, not quite, but they really wanted to talk about the subject. Because security was essential, I steered away any questions that got into details. They especially hate that their favorite author, which I must admit is me, is having her words censored. Maybe, hopefully, this upcoming FBI shindig will help the situation.

We had a ball as usual. Jenny Maxwell, age 79, is one of the leaders of the group. She proposed a toast: "My friends, let's raise our glasses to Melanie Pierce, the greatest novelist of our time. May she *pierce* the wall of censorship."

Have I mentioned that I love my girls?

Chapter 50

I had lunch with my BFF Sheila at the Brooklyn Diner on 57th Street, just a few blocks from Sheila's apartment. My writing is doing well—too well. The reason I say it's going too well is because it's only partially my writing. It's heavily edited by terrorist scumbags. Max is a doll, as always, and helps me with my emotional bullshit. Also, my girls couldn't be more supportive. But I'm gradually going nuts because I simply hate the idea that my words will be edited, not for good writing or accuracy, but for content which is not of my choosing.

Sheila gets it. She gets that I'm not satisfied even though my books sell like crazy. She knows that I take my profession seriously and not as a way to make a buck, even though I make a nice buck.

"This is going to go away, Mel. You know that. The entire government at all levels is going batshit over this censorship. And the part of the government that is especially on steroids is the FBI, the bureau where my favorite cousin and your husband is the star agent. As you well know, Max sees this as a direct attack on the most core part of our culture, freedom of speech. I didn't push you into a relationship with Max just because he's handsome and sweet. I knew that he's the kind of man who would appeal to a woman of your brains and ability. You're the real deal, Mel, and so is Max."

"Sheila, honey, you've been my best friend for years. Bringing me together with Max is the greatest thing you ever did for me, and I'll never forget it. Yes, Max and I are soulmates in every sense of the word. Although he can't tell me everything, I know he's on the case—big time. Sometimes I selfishly think that this is all my problem. Nothing can be farther from the truth. Max and the rest of the people at the Bureau look at this problem as a direct attack on our country. No, it's not just about me, although I constantly complain about it. It's about the very principles on which America was founded. I'm sorry I constantly bitch and moan about this. It's not just about me and my writer friends. It's about *any* writer, present and future. Yes, I realize it's all about the very friggin core of our democracy."

"Max, the FBI, and the NYPD will stop these bastards, Mel. You know they will and so do I."

Chapter 51

President Matt Blake sat in the Oval Office meeting with Jake Langstrom, his Chief of Staff, First Lady, Dee Blake, FBI Director Sarah Watson, and Senate Majority Leader, Wayne Tiverton. The topic of the meeting was *Editorial Terrorism.*

"Sarah, I understand that this goddam *Editorial Terrorism* crisis has taken a new turn," the President said. "Please bring us up to date."

"Yes, Mr. President, the situation has taken a dramatic new turn, and you wisely refer to it as a crisis. I believe it's the greatest crisis I've ever seen in all my years with the FBI. We all know the simple parts of this operation. Every author who has been contacted by that terrorist outfit known as The Committee is given a choice: either bow to their demands and submit every book for editorial review by the Islamic radicals or see a family member slain. But here's the shocker that I have to report today. As of two days ago, the demand isn't just to edit any content that's critical of radical Islam. The editing now includes elements having nothing to do with Islam at all. Two days ago, the eldest son of the famous novelist Barbara Langdon was killed, hacked to death with a machete. The book in question is *A Summer*

Surprise. Not only is the book without any criticism of Islam, it never even mentions any religion at all. The editorial terrorist's objection was to a love scene. You heard that right—a love scene. Here is the editor's note to Ms. Langdon: 'This scene is far too explicit. Your job as a writer is not to provide sexual titillation for heathen Infidels.' Barbara Langdon is well-known for writing steamy romance novels, and she is never hesitant to use blunt terms, including male and female body parts. The love scene in question, a scene between a *married couple*, quite explicitly mentions the partners' anatomies. So, Barbara Langdon simply deleted any mention of bodily members, but otherwise left the scene in the book. Then she made a critical mistake. She assumed, according to her statement to the FBI, that if she simply toned down the love scene it would be acceptable to the terrorist editor. She didn't resubmit the book to the radical editors and simply signed off on her rewritten scene to her publisher. Her grave mistake was not to resubmit the book to the jihadi editor and her eldest son paid with his life."

"Dear Lord," Dee Blake said. "I've written some scenes that could be described as 'steamy' in my books. I guess I'll need to make sure all my submissions are G Rated."

"It gets worse, a lot worse," Sarah Watson said. "The jihadi editors are starting to look at political statements. Here is one comment that was submitted to one of the writers last week: 'There is entirely too much Infidel heroism in this book. Refrain from making the Infidels look so heroic. They are heathen scum and do not deserve to be praised.' I spoke to Melanie Pierce, one of the finest novelists in the country in my opinion. Melanie, whose husband is an FBI agent, is beside herself. Her books are loaded with political content as well as adult love scenes. Like you, Madam First Lady, Melanie Pierce was inflicted with that *Veritas* drug to curb her writing. Thank God we found a cure, and you and Melanie are back with us."

President Blake stood and walked in front of his desk and then sat on top of it. It's a gesture he often uses to alert his guests that he has something important to announce.

"Our nation is under attack, it's that simple. War has been declared on us, not by a nation but by a group of thugs who think they can go after the basic core of American values, our freedom of speech. I'm not going to let that happen. I will assign a company of Navy SEALs to an upcoming meeting to provide backup support for a SWAT team operation, which I can't discuss further. I intend to win this war."

"But sir," Senate Majority Leader Langstrom said, "What about the Posse Comitatus Act. I'm sure that will preclude our use of SEALs in a civilian matter."

"Nothing in the act stops me from ordering a military unit to hold exercise maneuvers on American soil. And that's what I intend to order, maneuvers. If the SEALS are needed to step into action, I will suspend the Posse Comitatus Act by executive order, and I expect you will back me up in the Senate, Wayne."

"I will do just that, Sir."

"Folks, it's time to lock and load. We need to take our country back."

Chapter 52

Mellie and I sat on our terrace overlooking Central Park sipping after-dinner drinks. I reminded her to sip, not gulp, although she told me she felt like slugging down gin straight from the bottle.

"The shit has hit the fan, Max, big time. According to that article in the *Wall Street Journal*, the jihadi folks are now targeting love scenes and political matters. Where does that leave me? Maybe I should write children's books. That's what Janice McDonald has been doing since her husband got whacked. This is not the America where you and I grew up, honey. The United States Constitution may as well be a short story."

"I just finished editing your latest manuscript, honey. Your love scenes, which I help you with, are hotter than hell. And your political jibes are dead on target. But after what we've just read, I expect that your jihadi editor will have some strong comments and equally strong demands."

"I'm sure he will. I'll bet that jihadi creep never had a piece of ass in his life."

I cracked up. "You have such a picturesque way with the

English language, baby."

"I know you can't talk about it, but I hope you FBI guys have something big coming up, something big and violent. Just make damn sure *you're* not involved in any gunplay. I don't want my honey in danger, no matter how important the mission."

"Yes, we do have some big plans, and yes, I can't talk about it."

The phone rang and I picked it up.

"Yes, sir, yes of course. A pleasure speaking to you too. She's right here. I'll put her on."

"It's the President. He wants to speak to you, honey."

"The president of what?"

"The President of the friggin United States. Here, don't keep him waiting."

"Holy shit," Mellie announced as she grabbed the phone.

"Good evening Mr. President, Melanie Pierce here." I was glad Max toned down my drinking. Nothing like speaking to the leader of the free world while slurring your speech and hiccupping. "I'll put you on speaker, sir, so Max can listen in if you don't mind."

"Yes, definitely. I want Max to hear what I'm going to say."

"Thank you, sir."

"Melanie, the last time we spoke was when I called to commiserate with you on having come out from under that horrible *Veritas* drug. Then I put you on with First Lady Dee. Typical of Melanie Pierce, you went from newly recovered victim to concerned hero as you consoled Dee and helped her get it all together. Melanie, I'm not exaggerating when I say that you are the voice of American novelists. God knows, Dee never shuts up about you. I'm not telling what you don't already know, but this *Editorial Terrorism* crisis has grown to a proportion none of us evenly vaguely suspected. Not only are they censoring any negative references to Islam, but they're now editing out romantic scenes and political comments. The voices of American literature are being shut down, and I'm not going to tolerate it. Tomorrow I'm holding a press conference from the White House where I'll declare a National State of Emergency. I want you to be there with me, Melanie, and to say a few of your articulate words. Your face and your voice are well known to the American people, and I want you beside me as a spokesperson for the writers of America. You can invite "your girls" to sit in the viewing area, and of course your wonderful husband, Max. The American people need to hear from you, Melanie. Please accept."

"I don't see how I can turn you down Mr. President."

"I can't friggin believe this, Max. The President wants me to appear with him at a news conference. I mean, holy shit, I'll be on TV with President Blake."

"Mel, honey, I never tire of telling you how much I love you. And I want you to recognize something, whether you like it or not. You, Mellie, are one of the most important people in the country."

Chapter 53

Max called Babs Holden who in turn contacted all my girls to invite them to the press conference. Within an hour I was happy that 13 of them could make it. Babs' insistence that they all use texting makes for fast communicating.

I personally called Mom, who did a not-so-small freak-out when I asked her to attend the press conference.

When Max and I arrived at the White House we were escorted to the James S. Brady Press Briefing room where the press conference would be held. I was seated behind the President to his right, which meant that my puss would be plastered all over national TV as he spoke. I was nervous as hell, but managed to keep it all in. I wished that little Maggie could have been there to give me snuggle support.

President Blake, in his normal efficient fashion, brought the nation up to speed on the growing crisis of *Editorial Terrorism*.

"I will now call to the stand one of our nation's greatest writers, the famous novelist, Melanie Pierce."

All of my guests were coached to keep from saying anything.

It was hysterical to see a bunch of old ladies silently fist pumping the air when the President introduced me. I love my girls.

"Thank you, Mr. President, for giving me the opportunity to communicate not only with my fellow writers but with all freedom-loving Americans. As President Blake said, our nation is under attack, not with rockets and bombs, but with words, or rather the absence of words, the deletion of words. The attack consists of censorship, a muzzling of words that we writers live our lives for. The censorship consists of requiring all writers to submit their manuscripts to *Editorial Terrorists* who enforce their demands with violence and outright murder. If an author refuses to bend to the terrorists' demands, the result is the murder of a loved one, as we've seen with actual events. Under this violent regime, no reader in America can be sure if they're reading the words of an author or the version as edited by killers. We Americans love our First Amendment rights, but those rights are under violent attack daily. I hope and pray that our leaders can put a stop to this despicable attack on our Constitution. Thank you again for giving me the opportunity to speak, Mr. President."

My girls apparently misplaced their instructions to remain silent. They stomped their feet, clapped, and shouted loudly. Mom didn't join them. Instead she inserted two pinky fingers in her mouth and let go of an ear-piercing whistle. From the look on his face it appeared that President Blake enjoyed their outburst.

When Max and I got into our car for the trip to the airport, he looked at me, wearing a captivating smile, and grabbed my hand.

"I married well," he said, winking at me.

Chapter 54

Marjorie Baxter, my new assistant, is one of the most efficient people I've ever worked with. She's a short, pretty black woman, although slightly overweight. Marjorie is a bundle of energy and completes whatever task I assign her in amazingly short time. I hired her a month ago, after checking her stellar credentials. She'd worked with SWAT teams in the past and knew the drill. Buster and Rick Bellamy had tasked me with the job of finding a rental property in Saugerties, New York, as close as possible to the terrorist safe house. I gave Marjorie the location and told her we needed a house with a minimum of 2,000 square feet.

With a combination of luck and Marjorie's diligence, we found a place right next door to the safe house, 2,200 square feet on one floor with a full basement. It was a vacation home and was used by the owners only in the summer and it was now November. It took her a few minutes to research the contact information for the owners. She called on a secure phone we use for security and for secret missions like this. She told them she wanted to rent the place for a family reunion. She said the owners seemed to be happy to get a rental tenant in November. As instructed, Marjorie rented the place for a month to give us some wiggle room in case the meeting date was changed. Rick Bellamy dispatched a four-man team of agents who are accustomed to operating on cases like this. Our plan was to embed 50 agents, including 40 members of the SWAT team and 10 of the rest of us, including me, Rick, Buster, and assistants. The plan was to insert five agents per day so as not to call attention to a large operation. According to Imam Mike, the big meeting would be held in 10 days, so we began our insertion plan. Only one car would be used to drop the agents off five at a time. We didn't want a bunch of cars which would have called attention to us.

At one p.m. Agent Joseph Crowley came to my office for a planned meeting. Joe was a former Marine major and he would command the enhanced SWAT team. He was just shy of six feet tall and had the build of an athlete. He had a rugged face that seemed to indicate he'd seen a lot of action. If a face carried words, it would read: "Don't even think about fucking with me." A former combat Marine myself, I felt immediately comfortable with Major Joe Crowley. He had apparently researched me on Google and found out all about my military background, including my decorations. We had both served in Afghanistan but at different times.

"Captain Max," as he called me, "I enjoy working with proven ass kickers and that would certainly describe you. It's an honor to serve with you."

Easy guy to like. He had a pleasant way about him, but most importantly, he's tough as nails. That's good, because he's in for one hell of a tough assignment.

Chapter 55

Mellie and I got back to our New York apartment at 4:15 p.m. after Mellie's amazing press conference. Laurie Monahan, our apartment sitter and dog watcher, greeted us. She's a sweet gal, a senior English major at Columbia University. She lives right nearby with her parents, five blocks from our building. Laurie loves working for us. Whenever we'd be gone overnight, she gets her own huge bedroom. She also loves dogs, a job requirement. The major reason she enjoys working for us is that she wants to be a novelist, and absolutely adores Mellie and her books.

"Oh my God, Melanie. I watched you on TV this afternoon for your press conference with President Blake. You are officially my favorite human being."

Definitely a sweet kid.

"Thanks so much for your kind words, Laurie. You're right up there with my favorite people too. And little Maggie appears to be in love with you. You told me the last time you were working on a novel. How is it coming along?"

"I can't believe it, Melanie, but I've actually finished a first draft."

"I'll be happy to take a look at it for you, Laurie. Consider me a beta reader."

"Am I dreaming? Melanie Pierce wants to beta read my book? I can't possibly impose on you to do something like that."

"Hey, when I started out, I got a lot of friendly input from published authors. I'd be happy to read your manuscript. What's the book about?"

"It's about a famous author and her FBI agent husband."

"Yes, I *definitely* want to read that manuscript. Email the draft to me. You have my email address."

Laurie left, wearing a smile as wide as a city block.

"That was really nice of you to make that offer to Laurie," Max said. "I love that she referred to you as her favorite human being. That pretty accurately describes how I feel about you. I still can't get your press conference out of my mind. I wasn't kidding when I told you that you're one of the most important people in the country."

"Hey, stop with the flattery or I'm going to have to jump you."

"It isn't just flattery, it's the truth. American literature owes you a big one. Not that I mind if you jump me. Let me prepare dinner for my famous wife. Why don't you make us a couple of drinks."

"I have two words for you, honey."

"Only two? I love you is three words, so you've got my curiosity up. So, what are the two words?"

"Poison gas."

"Poison gas? What can you possibly be talking about?"

"Max, honey, you know that I understand that you can't tell me about what you're working on because of the 'need to know rule,' but you also know that I have the mind of a detective. From the bits and pieces of your phone conversations, I know that this meeting you've been talking about will be a violent attack of some sort. When I hear you use the words 'SWAT team,' I was convinced. My gut and my curious mind tells me that the FBI is planning a raid on a meeting of jihadis, specifically the bastards in charge of the *Editorial Terrorism* operation. Although that idea makes me happy as hell, the last thing in the world I want is for the love of my life to be involved in a shoot out with guns. It's a lot safer to poison the scumbags."

"Okay, honey, I'm done playing games with that need-to-know stuff. I'll tell you everything, because I trust you more than any person on earth. Besides that, you seem to have figured it out all by yourself. Yes, we are planning a raid, and I'm in charge of the logistics. We're going to attack a jihadi safe house in Saugerties, New York, ten days from now to be accurate. The actual raiding party will consist of 40 Enhanced SWAT team guys, trained killers. Sarah Watson will have overall command, but my old friend Buster, Director of the CIA, will have operational control. I know you've met Buster, but you don't know him as well as I do. One of his main objectives is to capture as many jihadis as possible to pump them for more information about the *Editorial Terrorism* operation. And when Buster wants information, he and his boys know how to get it. We want this to be the end of that goddam *Editorial Terrorism*. Our objective is to free you and the writers of America, and restore the First Amendment to its rightful place. If we use poison gas or something like that, we'll destroy evidence we may need for the future. This operation is under the watchful eyes of none other than the President of the United States. Don't worry about me, honey. I won't be directly involved in the raid, but if it comes my way, I know how to handle a gun, including an M 16."

"Take me with you, Max. Deputize me as a provisional FBI agent. Nobody knows better than me what those bastards are all about. I can be very helpful interrogating any prisoners."

"Now you've got me worried about you. I don't want you to be anywhere near gunplay."

"Max, honey, you know my idea makes sense. And I know how to handle a gun too."

"You're the best, baby. You're one great American. I'll talk to Buster about it. He's a big fan of yours, and I'm sure he'll agree. But this is a top-secret operation. Don't think you're going to write a novel about it."

"You're no fun. I'll mix us a couple of martinis."

Chapter 56

I have a hard time believing that Mellie is now a provisional FBI agent. Sarah Watson and Buster loved the idea of Mellie being involved in our sting operation. She knows the *Editorial Terrorism* scheme better than anyone.

Major Joe Crowley, head of the SWAT team, convinced me that his people should arrive in a large camper bus rather than be posted at our newly rented safe house. That was fine by me because it left some room in the house. Of the 10 of us who will be stationed in the house, five are women, including Mellie and Bobbie Nelson. The women will be assigned to two bedrooms. Although Mellie and I are married, as are Bob and Bobbie, this operation won't allow for marital togetherness.

We arrived in groups of five. As planned, only one car was involved because we didn't want to draw attention to our operation. Bob Crowley and his SWAT team were stationed two blocks away in a large camper bus. It was 9 p.m., the night before our planned attack. Buster was in the camper along with Rick Bellamy, leaving me in charge of our newly rented safe house. All

10 of us trained binoculars and telescopes on the target house.

"That house looks empty," Mellie said. "Not a light is on."

Just then my phone sounded. It was Buster.

"Max, I have Imam Mike on the line. I'll patch you in."

"Get out, get out, get out," Mike yelled. "They've changed the meeting place and nobody is there. You are about to be attacked by drones."

Bob Crowley ordered his camper bus to the house and pulled up next to the door.

"Everybody out and into the bus," I shouted. "NOW, right fucking now."

The bus pulled away. I looked out the rear window and saw the first drone rocket hit our safe house, followed by a constant barrage. The house was an exploding mass of fire. We'd just escaped with our lives. These Editorial Terrorists are killers.

Imam Mike gave Buster a new address for the jihadi meeting, a half hour away from our current location.

When we arrived at the new location, Bob Crowley ordered his 40 SWAT people to position themselves around the house, all of them equipped with heavy firepower. His men placed six large powerful lights around the perimeter, the purpose of which was to blind the people inside and provide cover for the agents on the lawn. They also placed four listening devices against windows. Buster wore earphones that were tuned to the devices. We wanted to make sure we had the right location.

"They're speaking Arabic," Buster said, "and I just heard the names of three of our targets. This is it. Lock & load, Major Bob."

Crowley put a microphone to his mouth and announced over a huge loudspeaker, "You are surrounded. Everyone come out with your hands in the air. If you do not comply immediately you will be destroyed."

Gunfire began to erupt from inside the house.

"Open fire," Crowley shouted.

The team opened up with MP5/10mm machine guns, M4 carbines, and six bazooka rocket launchers. I hadn't seen anything like this since Afghanistan.

After five minutes Crowley shouted, "Cease fire."

A man stood at the front door waving a white flag. Five others stood next to him, one bleeding heavily. Ten SWAT team members entered the house. We heard rapid gunfire. Apparently, some of the jihadis chose to resist. After an agonizing five minutes, the leader of the infiltration team shouted into his microphone, "The house is secure."

Ten FBI SUVs roared up to the scene as had been planned. The injured man was placed in one of the vehicles with a physician and nurse attending to him. Buster ordered everyone out of the camper bus, and we all ran to various SUVs. I was amazed that the operation worked at all because it was nothing like we originally planned. I then ordered the four remaining prisoners to be taken into the bus. I was standing next to Buster. Mellie walked up next to us and said, "I guess you want me to help with the interrogations."

"Thank you, Melanie, for your offer of assistance and for your courage," Buster said. "But we won't be needing your help. All we're looking for are other names of people who may be involved in this plot."

I knew exactly what Buster was up to. Although Mellie could

be of assistance, Buster wanted to perform his usual methods of interrogation. And the last thing he wanted were any witnesses to his "usual methods of interrogation."

We returned to New York for our post-operation debriefing which will be held at 26 Federal Plaza. I ordered 10 FBI agents to circulate among the SWAT team as well as the rest of us to take down written statements which would become part of the full report of the operation. At the FBI, we love paperwork.

Chapter 57

I told Marjorie Baxter, my talented new assistant, to contact all the authors who had been targeted by The Committee. I put out one simple directive: Contact your terrorist editor and send a manuscript for approval, no matter what state the manuscript was in. From our experience we knew that the turnaround time for a response to a manuscript was no longer than two days. Then began the wait. I added three days to the schedule for a total of five to be sure. The question that I wanted an answer to? Was there anything left to *Editorial Terrorism*?

Mellie and I returned to our apartment at 2 a.m. Laurie Monahan, our apartment/dog sitter, was asleep in her room, along with Maggie. We didn't want to wake her, nor did we have any desire for conversation. We were exhausted.

We showered and went to bed. Both of us fell immediately to sleep, wrapped in each other's arms but too tired to do what we wanted to do, make love.

We both woke at 6 a.m., still tired, but too wound up to

sleep any more. I was worried about Mellie. I've seen combat before, more than I want to remember, but yesterday was a new experience for Mellie. Will she be the same Mellie after the horror of yesterday?

We walked into the kitchen to have coffee. Marjorie had left a note at 5:30 a.m. saying she knew we must be tired, so she left. Class act that kid.

I called our favorite local deli to have breakfast delivered. Mellie and I had so much to talk about I didn't want either of us to be bothered with cooking. I had left a message at the office saying I would be taking off a couple of days. We definitely needed some time to decompress. When breakfast was delivered, we sat and ate at the kitchen counter, which was about the size of the State of Connecticut.

I was relieved and happy that Mellie seemed to be fine, just a bit tired. We took our third cups of coffee and sat in the den. Little Maggie seemed deliriously happy to be sitting on Mellie's lap. Mellie reached over and stroked my face.

"Yesterday I saw a different Max, honey. Besides being the wonderful man I love, I saw one hell of a tough military commander. I'm so proud of you, baby. If at all possible, I think I love you even more. How did Sheila put it? You're the real deal."

"I've been worried about you, Mellie. Yesterday you saw some really nasty shit, not the kind of stuff a writer encounters. But you seem to be just fine."

"Yes, it was nasty shit, but to be honest, with you next to me I felt totally safe. I love you, baby. You're my man, my everything. How about a hug?"

"I'm happy as hell to see you relaxed, baby. Hey, we may be all done with *Editorial Terrorism,* and we'll know for sure in a few days. Soon, please God, you will have command of your own mind, your own words."

"Hey, Max, do you know what's one of my favorite things in the world?"

"Writing a novel?"

"No, more than that. My favorite thing in the world is sex in the morning with my hunk of a husband. Let's go to bed and make it happen, baby."

Today is turning out a lot better than I expected.

Chapter 58

Five days later

Today is day five of Max's deadline for declaring that *Editorial Terrorism* is over. I was sitting in Max's office. Sarah Watson told Max that he should be the one to make the big announcement for all the amazing work he did on the *Silent Author Case*. Not one author reported that they had received any response to their manuscripts that were submitted to the editors of terror. Oh my God, I think it's over. The agreed time for the announcement was 4 p.m. My girls are going to freak out.

At 3:59, Sarah Watson called. "Let's hear it, Max. I hope Mellie is sitting next to you."

Max held the microphone, which was tied into the entire public address system. My heart was pounding like a jackhammer.

"Good afternoon, everyone. I'm happy to announce that *Editorial Terrorism* is over. Yes, it's over. We have our nation back. The writers of our country are now free to express their own thoughts, just as intended by the First Amendment. God bless our great country."

I threw my arms around him, always one of my favorite things to do. Among his many talents, Max has an amazing way of saying just the right words.

Max grabbed my hand and looked into my eyes.

"You're the greatest writer in the country, baby, maybe the world. You're no longer a silent author. Now that you're free to write your courageous words, tell me about your thoughts on your next novel."

"I'm thinking of a children's book, one about an adventurous family of cuddly puppies. Wadda ya think, honey?"

"Gimme a kiss, wiseass."

Characters – *The Silent Author*

Baxter, Marjorie – Max Wakefield's assistant

Bellamy, Ellen – TV Talk Show Host. Rick's wife

Bellamy, Rick – Head of FBI Counterterrorism Task Force. Ellen's husband

Buchanan, Nancy – FBI Agent

Busharif, Muhammed – Imam Mike

Buster – CIA Director, aka Charles Atkins, aka Gamal Akhbar

Chudori, Ali – Terrorist, aka Harry Paxton

Cranston, Madeline – Novelist

Crowley

Cummings, Rachel – Novelist

Hawkins, Michael – Melanie Pierce's pen name

Jackson, Sheila – Melanie's best friend

Langdon, Barbara – Novelist

Lawton, Bob – NYPD Detective

Maloney, Janice – Novelist, Pulitzer Prize winner

McDonald, Janice – Novelist whose husband was murdered

McGraw, Bob – FBI Agent

McMartin, Trevor – Bank examiner

Melton, Jack – Melanie's literary agent

Milburn, Jason – Amagansett Police Chief

Miller, Bob – FBI Agent and Max's assistant

Monahan, Laurie – Max and Mellie's house sitter.

Myers, Frank – Director of FBI research lab

Nelson, Bobbie – NYPD Detective

Paxton, Harry – Embezzler and terrorist, aki Ali Chudori

Peterson, John – Physician at Columbia Presbyterian Hospital

Pierce, Hedda – Melanie's mother

Pierce, Melanie – Novelist

Samson, Rick – Episcopal Priest, friend of Max

Thompson, Jacqueline – Novelist

Tiverton, Wayne – Senate Majority Leader

Townsend, Walter – FBI lab science researcher

Wakefield, Debbie – Max's sister, NYPD Detective

Wakefield, Max – FBI Agent, Melanie Pierce's husband

Watson, Sarah – FBI Director

Weinberg, Bennie – Detective and psychiatrist

THE BOOKS OF RUSS MORAN

I hope you enjoyed reading *The Long Island Project as* much as I enjoyed writing it. As many a Long Islander, I have spent time "stuck" on Long Island, the result of a traffic jam. I'll never forget the time when the Verrazano Bridge, the Throgs Neck Bridge, the Whitestone Bridge, and the George Washington bridge were all shut down hard. As I drummed my fingers on the steering wheel, I did what most novelists do – I looked for a story, or rather I noticed that a story had found me. What if Long Island was quarantined with no way on or off? By the time I eventually found my way to New Jersey, a story had formed in my head, *The Long Island Project*.

This book, as well as all my books are available on Amazon. com, and also as ebooks on The Kindle or a Kindle app on your smartphone or iPad.

The Gray Ship – **Book One of** *The Time Magnet Series*
http://amzn.to/16GPumH

A number one Amazon best seller. "This provocative, intensely powerful novel is a must-read for sci-fi fans and Civil War aficionados, though mainstream fiction readers will find it heart-rending and inspiring as well. A rare read that's not only *wildly entertaining, but also profoundly moving.*" – Kirkus Reviews

The Thanksgiving Gang – **Book Two of** *The Time Magnet Series*
http://amzn.to/1NzBs7N

The Sequel to *The Gray Ship.* A story of time travel.

"I had never read a book before written in an efficient,

minimalistic prose. Instead of writing what most readers want to read, he gives voice to life-like characters, with their flaws and prejudices. They are not infallible superheroes. It's always nice to find a new voice in fiction and to enjoy creativity at its best." — C. Ludewig.

"Breakneck pacing and virtually nonstop action" – Kirkus Reviews

A Time of Fear – Book Three of *The Time Magnet Series*
http://amzn.to/1zdjaG9

In a month, five American cities will be devastated by suitcase nuclear bombs.

The time travelers take on their old name, *The Thanksgiving Gang*.

-They know what will happen, because they travelled to the future.

-They know what the result will be. They've seen the devastation.

-They know the details. Five American Cities targeted by nuclear suitcase bombs.

-BUT they don't know where the bombs are—and they don't know how to find them.

The clock is ticking, and millions will soon lose their lives – unless they find the bombs.

"His story is fascinating, and adds even more depth to this already cavernously deep novel. Amazingly unique, chilling and well written, Moran weaves a future that is both desperate and hopeful. Blending modern fears with science fiction results in a tale that will keep you reading long into the night. Five stars!" – Heather

The Skies of Time – **Book Four of** *The Time Magnet Series*
http://amzn.to/1CCC3jg

In *The Skies of Time*, you will recognize the two main characters, Ashley Patterson, now an admiral, and her husband, Jack Thurber. They met and fell in love in *The Gray Ship*, and now they're in for the adventure of their lives in *The Skies of Time*. Ashley and Jack have been such prominent characters in all four books of The Time Magnet Series that I feel like they're old friends. You will also recognize some of the other characters. But if I told you who they are, it would ruin the fun.

"I'm big fan of this series and this one may be the best. I hope there is another book to this series since it keeps getting better. There are a few questions I have about certain events that makes the next one even more suspenseful. These are great books to binge read one after the other." – Time Travel Fan

The Shadows of Terror – **Book One of the** *Patterns Series*
http://amzn.to/1IDQzJS

A stunning page turner. A novel that explodes off the front page of your newspaper.

Terrorism has a new face, a face that's obscured in the shadows. The radical forces of destruction have learned to make themselves invisible to the West, and preventing a terrorist attack has become almost impossible.

A new war has begun, World War III.

Rick Bellamy, an FBI agent who specializes in counterterrorism, is engaged in his own war, a war with no end.

Bellamy's wife, Ellen, a prominent architect, discovers that she's in the middle of the greatest terror plot to date.

To defeat the enemy, Bellamy first has to uncover the clues, to shine a light on the shadows. He has to find patterns – before it's too late.

"Move over James Patterson and Mary Higgins Clark. There's a new guy in town. Russ Moran's new book – *The Shadows of Terror.*" – Frank O.

The Scent of Revenge - Book Two in the *Patterns Series*
http://amzn.to/1UvDRmw

The world is at war with the forces of terror. FBI Agent Rick Bellamy and his wife, Ellen, find themselves in the middle of a sinister terrorist plot.

Someone is attacking young prominent women, inflicting a horrible disease.

Nobody knows its origin, nobody knows how to stop it, nobody knows how to cure it.

Rick Bellamy and a team of scientists want to go on the offense. But how?

Will the lives of the women be changed forever? When will the attacks stop?

"Heart pounding, can't put down thriller that will force you to look at terrorism in different light. Life in America will never be the same." – Cold Coffee Cafe

Sideswiped - Book One in the Matt Blake series of legal thrillers.
http://amzn.to/1MkxX35

Trial lawyer Matt Blake took on a perfect case.

It involved a sideswipe collision in which his client's husband, an investigative reporter, was killed. The evidence of negligence was overwhelming. Eyewitnesses testified that defendant was talking on his cell phone when he hit the other car.

But was it negligence? Was it an accident?

Or was it murder?

Matt uncovers evidence that the act may have been intentional. Somebody wanted the man silenced. Somebody wanted the man dead.

Somebody had a lot to hide.

The signs started to point to the highest levels of government.

An open-and-shut personal injury case suddenly became a vast conspiracy of terror.

"This book hooks you in from the first line. *Sideswiped* draws you into the world of Matt Blake and you become emotionally attached to him and his journey. The story itself is so well-written and moves quickly. There is never a dull moment." – Sarah Elle

"Moran demonstrates the depth of his writing talent by developing a new genre with *Sideswiped*, a legal thriller. Branching out from his previous novels dealing with time travel, Moran goes in a whole new direction with Book One in the Matt Blake series. He creates a wild but totally believable story of modern day intrigue and suspense. Moran also deftly weaves into this book some of my favorite characters from his prior novels. I am looking forward to starting Book #2 - *The Reformers* – Frank from Lynbrook on August 16, 2016

The Reformers - **Book Two of the Matt Blake Series of legal thrillers, is the sequel to** *Sideswiped.*
ttp://amzn.to/2m8uMdu

The forces of radical Islam are on the run.

Their leadership has been decimated, their ranks thinned, their power disappearing by the week.

Their recruiting efforts have been cut off, the radical websites shut down, and the attraction of jihad is losing its appeal among the young.

With targeted assassinations, military strikes, as well as the loss of oil fields and gold mines, radical Islam is fast losing power.

But who is responsible?

It isn't the United States Government. It's a new force the world has never seen before.

Lawyer Matt Blake and his wife Diana find themselves in the middle of the most gigantic plot the world has ever seen, a conspiracy that's only begun to grow.

"I've been a fan of the author, Russell Moran, since reading *Sideswiped* a few months ago, so I admittedly went into this book with quite high expectations. That being said, I had no idea that "*The Reformers*" was going to play out in the way that it does and I can see myself giving this book a re-read in the future. In fact, I am even more impressed by the storyline of this read than the last and it has left me excited to see more." – Lucidity.

The Keepers of Time - **Book Five of the** *Time Magnet Series*
http://amzn.to/2wjVSTt

Admiral Ashley Patterson and her husband Jack have done it

again. They've traveled through time, 200 years into the future – aboard a nuclear aircraft carrier, Ashley's flagship.

They discover a new world, a strange new world – a post-nuclear war world – one that is both a beacon of hope, and a cry of despair.

They meet a group of people who call themselves *The Keepers of Time,* an organization dedicated to preserving history and culture amid the horrors of a dystopian future.

The world around them has harkened back to a primitive and savage past, one that includes human sacrifice.

Ashley knows they must have to get back to the present to warn the government of the unspeakable horrors that await. But finding the way back to the present is their greatest challenge, an almost insurmountable one.

"The Keepers of Time is a really interesting take on current geopolitical events and where they are leading. From reading previous books in the series, the cast of characters is as familiar as the people next door and it was great to reconnect with them. Moran's legal background illuminates what happens when our legal structure disappears, and he has zeroed in on an essential thing about civilization – records of the past. A great read!" Robert Shearer

"Time flies when you're scared out of your mind. The author's superb writing skills will quickly draw you into the story. Forty-two fast paced chapters will keep turning the pages of this novel until the end. Well-developed cast of realistic characters that you will relate to one will keep you engaged. One of my favorite things about Moran's books is his entire cast of characters detailed in the back of the book. I admit to reading about the cast first in order to firmly get everyone in my mind. As a follower of his, I know each character is important to the plot and I don't want to miss anything or overlook anyone." – Cold Coffee

"A wild time travel yarn that starts fast and doesn't slow down until the end."

A Reunion in Time
http://amzn.to/2tneIsg

What if a 37-year-old adult travels back 20 years in time and finds himself in high school, followed by his 36-year-old wife? They're now teenagers, 17 and 16.

Adults in teenage bodies, they struggle to convince the people from their past that they are real, not apparitions. With the benefit of hindsight, they know the history of the past 20 years, and it isn't pretty.

Rick and Ellen are married, and now have to adjust to married life as teenagers in 2001. Rick is a senior FBI official and Ellen is a famous architect.

But everybody sees them as kids. Nobody believes that they're married, and nobody believes their stories—until Rick and Ellen predict 9/11.

How do they find their way back to the year they came from? How do they warn the authorities of the cataclysm that will occur in the future? The answer is to find the time portal—the wormhole—that brought them to 2001. But the site has changed. It's no longer the place where they crossed the wormhole. Will they live out the balance of their lives beginning as teenagers?

"We've all wished we could go back to earlier times with the mind we have now. This Russell Moran book takes you there and it is a fun creative romp well worth reading. *A Reunion in Time* is highly recommend!" – Kindle Customer.

The President is Missing – Book Three of the Matt Blake series.
http://amzn.to/2t9v7wu

While he was addressing the nation from a submerged nuclear submarine, President Blake's message is suddenly cut off. Anyone listening heard an explosion. The explosion was followed by floating debris five minutes later.

First Lady Dee Blake has doubts, which she shares with naval high command and the new president. She thinks the explosion and the debris were a ruse to make people think the sub was destroyed, and her husband with it.

Could the sub have been hijacked and the president kidnapped?

But who would commit such an act? What is its purpose?

Was it Russia, China, Iran, or a shadowy group of freelance terrorists?

The new president appoints Dee as his Chief of Staff, with explicit instructions to find the missing submarine—and President Matt Blake.

Her life, and the life of the nation, suddenly take a horrifying turn.

"Russ Moran wrote a true thriller, with a strong plot and even stronger characters. To think that there are good guys - Russian Naval Admirals, no less - made this book not only a solid who-done-it but also a strong 'why did they do it?' " – Unka Heshie

Robot Depot
http://amzn.to/2zXW7C2

Mike Bateman is a visionary businessman, the creator and CEO of the fabulously successful chain of stores, Robot Depot, a company dedicated to selling robots and Artificial Intelligence machines for a variety of uses.

The company is a darling of Wall Street and is the most popular destination for consumers and businesses looking for labor saving devices.

But the company caught the eye of ISIS, the terrorist Islamic State. They discover a great way to deliver bombs – using the products of Robot Depot to kill people.

Robot Depot changed from being a popular company to an object of fear because of the tampered products it sells. The terrorists use the company for "terror spectaculars," including the destruction of a skyscraper, a drone attack on Yankee Stadium, and the bombing of a children's sailing regatta.

Mike Bateman and the FBI are in a race to stop his products from becoming weapons, a race to stop the wanton killings. His wife and partner, Jenny, discovers the true meaning of terror one horrible summer day.

"Moran just got a new fan. This is the first book of Moran's that I've read, but I look forward to reading more of his work. I enjoyed this story, and found that Moran is not only a good writer, but he's a good storyteller as well. It's an interesting and creative story, mixing new technology and AI uses, with terrorism. It's a thriller that keeps the reader turning the page, and it's extremely captivating. I enjoyed the story and look forward to future works of his." Amy's Bookshelf

A Climate of Doubt
https://amzn.to/2OSwcHR

Forget what you ever heard about climate change.

Forget your preconceived notions about reality itself.

Instantly, you are in a new world, a horrifying world, a world you don't understand.

On a hot summer day, Homeland Security Secretary, Rick Bellamy, and his wife Ellen, a famous TV talk show host, walked along the ocean front trying to escape the heat. Suddenly the temperature dropped from the high 90s to below freezing in a matter of minutes. It began to snow – *on July 16*.

The temperatures across the country and the world plummeted, creating winter in summer.

Bellamy and the rest of the government struggled to cope with the suddenly new climate, but to cope, they first had to find out what happened.

Scientists from academia blamed the weather on a sudden acceleration of climate change, but they were unable to explain a 60-degree temperature drop in a matter of minutes.

Two astronauts in an American space station realized that the sudden weather calamity coincided with a test of the 20 satellites that the space station controlled.

Attention focused on a huge American corporation that owned the space station and the satellites. Could there be a connection between the satellite tests and the radical drop in temperature?

As the deaths piled up and the world economy tilted toward disaster because of gigantic summer blizzards, Rick Bellamy and his team struggled to find answers before it was too late. Was it a sudden shift in climate change or did it have something to do with the satellites? The biggest question remained – was the catastrophe an accident, or was somebody controlling the weather? Was it terror?

Bundle up and get this page-turning thriller. You're in for a wild ride. The book was published in May of 2018. It's Book Four of the Matt Blake Series. Matt and Dee Blake take on their biggest challenge to date, along with our old friends, Rick and Ellen Bellamy.

"Mr. Moran does a masterful job of crafting an action-packed, suspenseful read about the devastating consequences of climate manipulation. The diabolical mastermind behind the caper is a dictator of the worst kind—a man without conscience who cares only for power. Through the magic of Mr. Moran's digital pen, the men and woman in white hats are three-dimensional and vividly real. While this is a work of fiction, it's plausible fiction. We can easily relate to the horrific consequences of such an act of terrorism as so capably portrayed in Mr. Moran's prose." – Colorado Avid Reader

The Maltese Incident – A Story of Time Travel **(Book One of the Harry and Meg Series), the prequel to** *The Violent Sea.*
https://amzn.to/2RclZCT

You're on a beautiful cruise ship.

The April sky is full of stars.

Suddenly, the ship rumbles, and instantly the stars disappear.

"What the hell was that?" Captain Fenton yelled.

"Beats me, captain. I've never seen anything like it," the first officer said.

They would soon discover that the ship, *The Maltese*, had just traveled through time – millions of years to the past.

The captain, Harry Fenton, a highly decorated naval war hero, realizes the greatest battle of his life lay ahead of him.

Captain Harry, a widow, falls in love with a beautiful passenger, Meg Johnson, an executive with the company that owns the ship.

After a whirlwind romance, they marry – in the ship's ballroom—100 million years in the past.

Captain Harry convinces the passengers and crew that they must move ashore to a tropical island because the ship is running out of fuel and supplies. He organizes a group to go ashore and inspect the island.

An ancient forest inhabited by dinosaurs awaits them.

Meg wants to go with them. Harry, fearing for her safety, tries to convince her to stay on the ship.

Meg demonstrates that she is proficient with a gun by taking apart a rifle and reassembling it – in 15 seconds. Harry marvels that he's never seen such an expert gun handler – or accurate shooter. So, AR-15 in hand, Meg joins the inspection party. Charging dinosaurs are no match for Meg Fenton's firepower.

Will the 1,000 souls ever make it back to the time they came from, or will they remain stranded in the distant past?

A scientist aboard theorizes that, to return to their present time, they need to go back to the time portal, or wormhole, that brought them to the past.

But the ship doesn't have enough fuel for the journey.

Realizing that their lives have hit the reset button, the crew and passengers construct a community in the forest – Malta Town.

Under Harry and Meg's leadership, they create a court system, a legislature, and all the elements of a small budding democracy. Meg figures out a way to harness hydroelectric power from a nearby waterfall. Everybody thinks of Harry and Meg as the heart and soul of Malta Town. They begin their new lives – among the dinosaurs.

The Maltese Incident is a riveting tale of time travel, love, courage, and horror.

Get this page turner now and prepare for the ride of your life.

"As with Moran's work, he continues to be a great storyteller. I recommend reading this from title to end. It's well written, and filled with intensity and levity." – Amy's Bookshelf

The Violent Sea – A Story of Time Travel
Book Two of the *Harry and Meg Series,* the sequel to
The Maltese Incident.
https://amzn.to/2AT5ypI

The Violent Sea is a novel of war, time travel, military history. It's the second book in the Harry and Meg Series. It's also a sweet romance between Harry and his wife, Meg.

Rear Admiral Harry Fenton has done it again. He's traveled through time to a different era. He finds himself, with a serious head injury from a fall, at Pearl Harbor Base Hospital on May 16, 1942, three weeks before the Battle of Midway. His wife and aide, Lieutenant Meg Fenton, is worried sick, and waits for him—in 2018.

Admiral Harry is the commanding officer of Carrier Strike Group 14 in 2018, but the people in 1942 think he's a busted-up hallucinating sailor who imagines himself an admiral.

Admiral Raymond Spruance is commanding officer of Carrier Task Force 16. After hearing about Harry's time travel stories, Spruance orders him brought to his flagship, the *USS Enterprise*.

After Harry tells him about his time travel experiences, Spruance is convinced the man is insane.

But after speaking to him at length, Spruance is amazed at Harry's knowledge of naval tactics and strategy. He calls Harry's bluff and orders him to stay aboard the *Enterprise* for her upcoming engagement at the Battle of Midway.

By the end of the battle, Spruance is convinced Harry is an admiral, and thinks of him as a friend.

Now Harry needs to figure out how to travel back to 2018, to his carrier command, but most importantly, to the love of his life, Lieutenant Meg.

After Harry returns to the present, the Fentons are deployed on Harry's flagship, the *USS Gerald R. Ford.* The ship encounters another wormhole, this one in the ocean. They are transported to 1944 and participate in the Battle of Leyte Gulf.

The book took me 10 months to write. It went through 20 drafts and three rounds with my editors. I did copious research for the book to ensure its historical accuracy. If you enjoy the genre of time travel, I think you will love this book. I got to know my two main characters in the prequel, *The Maltese Incident.* Harry and Meg are deeply in love but enjoy constant banter and wisecracks. One of my favorite characters, Admiral Ashley Patterson of *The Gray Ship,* makes an important cameo appearance in *The Violent Sea.*

"What a great book. You will love this book. Time travel telling at its best. At the end you will believe it is possible. Russell Moran has crafted a great continuation from *The Maltese Incident* his character development has continued from the first book throughout this book and possibly beyond. His writing is so detail oriented you will find yourself believing that time travel is not only real but possible. This book was given to me as a gift but it turned out to be one of the greatest gifts I have ever received. You will find that your investment of money and time reading this book to be a great investment. Time and money both well spent." – Mike the Mailman

A Sea of Fear – **A Novel of Time Travel**
Book 3 of The Harry and Meg Series.
https://amzn.to/2GERuSx

You're Five-Star Admiral Harry Fenton, whom President Blake calls the greatest fighting admiral in American history.

Along with your Navy Commander wife, Meg, you lead your carrier strike group against the worst enemy the country has faced since World War II, a small nation that is intent on destroying the world's shipping industry. The seas of the world have become scenes of plunder, pillage, and mass murder.

The president has convinced you to come out of retirement and put an end to the looming crisis. He promotes you to Fleet Admiral, the highest-ranking officer since Admiral Chester Nimitz.

You and Meg were having a pleasant retirement, running a world-class resort that you bought in Rhode Island. But when the president pleads you to "Give 'em Hell, Harry," you know that you can't ignore his call to duty.

As people who have time traveled in the past, you come up with an idea to travel three years into the future. With President Blake's blessing, you and Meg lead a group of officers into the future. What you find is horrifying, an America taken over by a totalitarian dictator.

You return to the past and report your findings. President Blake, hearing your terrifying story, convinces you that you have an even bigger call to duty, the greatest challenge of your life.

You take on the challenge for one reason—Meg will be at your side.

As in the first two books of the Harry and Meg Series, *The Maltese Incident* and *The Violent Sea, A Sea of Fear* is a sweet romance between two of literature's most exciting and likable characters, Harry and Meg Fenton.

A Sea of Fear is a story of war, politics, time travel, and love.

"This story is incredible. I felt like it was real-life and happening NOW! The way the political world is unfolding with the lies and innuendos, something like this could be possible. The main couple, husband and wife, Meg and Harry worked together to solve and help the nation climb onto its rock-solid feet. Surely this is the integrity that the United States government stands for. They had me in their corner wanting to see them win against the evil Antonio Martin. Read the story, it will enthrall and pull you in as it did me...Great ending." – Cristella

Leonardo Murphy – A Coming of Age Thriller
https://amzn.to/31vzC4S

You just launched a satellite into space without a rocket.

You invented a computer algorithm that writes novels.

You just entered Harvard University on a full scholarship after completing high school in two years.

Not bad for a 12-year-old kid.

Leonardo changed his name from William to Leonardo to honor his hero, Leonardo da Vinci. Young Leonardo Murphy has the second highest IQ ever recorded.

Leonardo, now 25, met a beautiful young woman named Janice, and fell madly in love. They married a year later.

Janice and Leonardo, who she calls "Lee," collaborate on various projects with the CIA and FBI.

But their intelligence activities put a target on their backs. They narrowly escape four assassination attempts.

Leonardo Murphy is a breathtakingly fast coming-of-age thriller about one of the most fascinating characters you will ever meet in literature. Instantly, you are shoulder to shoulder with the world's most amazing genius.

"Finally, a believable super hero comes to life! Peaks and valleys of horrific actions are neatly juxtaposed against comic relief. The humor, ranging between the poles of mild to downright hysterical, will surely tickle your funny bone. The frequent use of the protagonist's favorite word (26 matches found throughout), which I won't divulge, would ordinarily belabor one's prose, save when Leonardo employs the term. As a matter of fact, the story concludes with that very word, but rather endearingly. No, I did not ruin the ending for you folks. You'll see." – Robert Banfelder

The Pineaire Incident – Book 4 of the Harry and Meg Series
https://amzn.to/2VXQ2lp

One hundred gigantic fast submarines suddenly appear in the ocean.

President Harry Fenton and his First Lady, Meg are shocked by the event, as are all the leaders of the world.

Where are the submarines from? What do they want? What are their intentions?

Six Russian submarines attack one of the mystery subs. All six Russian subs are destroyed in two minutes.

President Fenton, along with Meg, reaches out to contact the leader of the strange fleet. They are amazed to discover that the subs are from another planet, Planet Pineaire.

But they're pleased to find out that the Pinearians came in peace, and bring with them an amazing gift, a new type of fuel that can revolutionize life on earth.

Get ready for an interplanetary thrill ride. *The Pinaire Incident* is Book 4 of the Harry and Meg series.

"Right at the beginning, we learn that 100 giant submarines are discovered with no idea how they could all suddenly appear. Being familiar with Harry & Meg, I immediately presumed they must have Time Traveled from some future time. Uh Oh, I almost gave away an important detail. You should already know that Harry and Meg are President and First Lady having recently defeated a small rogue nation that destroyed the Cruise Ship industry and nearly took over the world's Shipping Industry. You might think peaceful times are ahead when abruptly, 100 of these 1,800 foot long submarines appear. Five Stars" – The Holey One

Puzzles Book 1 – A Detective Love Story
https://amzn.to/2MI6TEo

Veteran police detectives Bobbie Nelson and Bob Lawton are partnered. They're both concerned that they may not get along. They're both highly skilled and love their work—They love to solve puzzles. They soon learn that they don't just love their jobs, they love each other. *Puzzles* is an action-packed police thriller wrapped around a sweet romance.

Bobbie and Bob are two of the most exciting and likeable characters you will find in literature.

"This book should be kept out of the hands of crooks, criminals, terrorists, and any others planning to do evil. There are so many techniques utilized by skilled detectives that are revealed that this book could be used as a training guide by the Bad Guys. Even so, the reality is that fundamental police work is what solves most crimes. Gathering and evaluating massive amounts of data and looking for patterns or repeating details is what our two main characters excel at." – The Holey One

"Russell Moran has done it again with Puzzles: A Detective Love Story. Each case builds upon earlier ones, with the BBs fine-tuning their puzzle-solving techniques to such a degree it's not long before the FBI and CIA reach out them to piece together more complicated scenarios impacting on society. Russell has created an easy-to-read and fast-paced story, which will keep you turning the pages late into the evening to find out what happens next. I can't wait for the next book in the series!" – R. J. Krzak

Puzzles, Book 2 – A Detective Love Story
https://amzn.to/3bmiqEh

The further adventures of Detectives Bob Lawton and Bobbie Nelson, now married.

The Long Island Project
https://amzn.to/2WgJC2n

Our old friends, Detectives Bobbie Nelson and Bob Lawton, "the BBs," are engaged in the most frightening case of their career, an armed quarantine of Long Island by a sinister group. To find the answer to the problem, they travel through time to 1942, and discover the problem is larger than they had thought. "A page turning thriller."

----⯎ ◆ ⯎----

About the Author

In addition to the 21 novels listed in the preceding pages, I also published five nonfiction books: *Justice in America: How it Works – How it Fails; The APT Principle: The Business Plan That You Carry in Your Head; Boating Basics: The Boattalk Book of Boating Tips; If You're Injured: A Consumer Guide to Personal Injury Law; How to Create More Time*. My latest nonfiction book is *The Novel - A Writer's Guide - Discover the Joy of Writing Fiction* published in November 2018.

I'm a lawyer and a veteran of the United States Navy. I live on Long Island, New York, with my wife and editor, Lynda, a Shih-Tzu named Sammie, and a Golden Retriever named Maggie.

A Personal Request

I hope you enjoyed reading *The Silent Author* as much as I enjoyed writing it. Max and Melanie are now two of my favorite characters. I think of them as old friends. You will be seeing more of them in future books.

Please consider leaving a brief review on amazon.com. It doesn't need to be lengthy or elaborate, just your thoughts on the characters, the scenes, and the story. Book reviews are the lifeblood of an author.

----⯎ ◆ ⯎----

www.ingramcontent.com/pod-product-compliance
Lightning Source LLC
Chambersburg PA
CBHW070004260626
47159CB00005B/1659